MW00876558

UNHEROIC: BOOK ONE

© 2017 Marcus V. Calvert

By Tales Unlimited, LLC.

For permissions, contact:
https://squareup.com/store/TANSOM.

Cover by Lincoln Adams

Edited by Ed Buchanan

ACKNOWLEDGEMENTS

I'd like to thank Ed Buchanan (my editor) for his expertise, steady support, and blunt-force candor.

I'd also like to thank Lincoln Adams (my cover artist) for his time, patience, and wicked-awesome skill.

Rose, thanks for keeping me in the game.

To everyone else who had a hand in this twisted thing being written (living or not), I thank you.

I must also tip a hat to my fellow artists and strangers-turned-fans. You truly are a hip crowd.

TABLE OF CONTENTS

THREE WISHES

Nick Mebliss drunkenly staggered down a darkened stretch of North Carolina beach. The college sophomore wore large khaki shorts, beer-stained leather sandals, and a black X-men t-shirt over his chubby frame. Snugly fitted around his curly brown head was a pink silk thong. In his right hand was a nearly-empty bottle of whiskey. Sounds of loud rap music raged from the beach house a quarter-mile behind him, where Day 3 of a four-day "Keggerfest" was about to end. Having lost most of his Spring Break money at poker, Nick decided to take a stroll along the beachfront and find a quaint little spot to throw up. He plopped down on a wet patch of sand and let the waves caress his feet.

Feeling nauseously serene, Nick sat back and eyed the clear night sky and its infinite array of stars. As a wave came in, something washed up alongside him. To his booze-blurred vision, it looked like a magic lamp. The golden object was heavy and encrusted with multi-faceted jewels. It also hummed with some kind of unseen power. With a giggle, Nick picked the lamp up and rubbed it three times—more as a joke than for any rational purpose.

A bald djinn suddenly appeared.

Stern-faced and regal, the djinn wore hooded red armor with a scimitar along his back. A mix of leather and chainmail, the armor fit loosely over his massive frame. Freed after countless centuries, the djinn breathed in the ocean air and thanked Nick for freeing him. Too drunk to be scared, Nick gave the djinn "props" on his wardrobe.

In his day, the djinn would've lopped Nick's head clean off. Instead, honor demanded that he offer the mortal three wishes as a reward. Barely conscious, Nick babbled them forth. Amused by the implications, the djinn granted each one with a chuckle (especially the first two).

Then he opened a white dimensional portal. When Nick asked where it led, the mythical being muttered something to the effect of: "Someplace sane." With a polite nod, the djinn departed. Nick waved goodbye as the ovular portal closed. Then he puked up some of the chili he had eaten earlier. Instead of heading back to the beach house, Nick took the opportunity to pass out.

The first explosion made Nick groan with minor annoyance. The smell of beer was stronger than that of his dried vomit. It seemed to come from everywhere.

The second explosion annoyed him even more.

"Kill the TV, willya'?!" Nick grumbled.

The third explosion was close enough to pepper him with sand. That's when Nick sat up and winced at the morning sun above. In spite of his thundering hangover, his eyes widened at the sight before him. The blue-green ocean waters were now beer-colored! It took him a few seconds to realize that it wasn't a chemical spill of some kind. The Atlantic Ocean—for as far as his eyes could see—had been turned to beer!

Nick's jaw dropped with thoughtless joy. Free beer was free beer, regardless of the circumstances. He reached down to scoop some up when a fourth explosion knocked him down. Dazed, he turned around and gawked some more.

Comic book heroes were slugging it out with comic book villains! Dozens of them were fighting all around him. They were all flesh-and-blood, down to their assorted costumes (most of which were spandex-based).

He recognized almost all of the combatants: from the noble ArgoKnight to the downright evil FemiNazi. Some had brute strength, others had energy blasts, and more than a few fought with assorted weaponry. From the way things were looking, the heroes were outnumbered four-to-one . . . and they were losing?! That never happened in the comics!

Nick wondered what the slugfest was about.

Gorilla Girl ran toward him on all fours. The green-furred mutated heroine dodged a few energy blasts, stray gunfire, and a mystical fireball. Just as she was about to tell Nick something, Gorilla Girl got blindsided by a well-thrown hammer. Ribs cracked, she went flying. Nick spotted the black metal hammer, which landed near her broken form. It vaguely resembled a blacksmith's hammer—only larger—with multiple gadgets built into it. One of them allowed the hammer to fly right back into the hand of its creator.

The nine-foot-tall cyber-barbarian wielded the hammer with his left hand and a massive, single-edged axe in his right. Bladehammer sneered at Nick, and then moved in on Gorilla Girl, who tried to crawl away. Unable to help her, Nick could only avert his eyes as the axe came down. Savoring the next kill, Bladehammer turned a wild eye toward Nick.

"Dyin' time, kid," Bladehammer began to gloat . . . only to break out into a sudden fit of uncontrollable sneezing.

Neither of them knew that Gorilla Girl's fur induced violent allergic reactions to 1-in-2,000 people. Undaunted, the villain breathed through his mouth and continued to advance. Among the debris and nearby corpses, Nick felt the butt end of a large raygun-like weapon. He desperately grabbed it.

Bladehammer rushed in with barbaric battle cry. Nick closed his eyes and pulled the trigger. The weapon's bluish beam of energy hit Bladehammer square in the chest, encasing him in ice. After the shot, the weapon's barrel emitted a smoking white gas, which cooled the surrounding air by thirty degrees. Caught in his violent pose, the only things that Bladehammer could move were his eyes, which angrily followed Nick as he stood up.

"Sweet!" Nick grinned as he got up.

Aping Bladehammer's cocky sneer, Nick pulled the trigger again. The young man's grin died when the weapon beeped a red light (indicating an empty power cell). As Nick uttered profanities and tossed the gun over his left shoulder, DarkHound raced straight at him from behind. Zipping through the raging battle, the crimson-skinned hellhound had six legs and a barbed tail. Nick never saw the beast coming.

Then the raygun landed in DarkHound's path. The hellhound stopped in its tracks, seized by an unbreakable urge. The only thing it liked more than tearing apart human flesh was the cold; something not very abundant in its native hell. The bloodthirsty hellhound affectionately curled up around the cold object and whimpered with joy.

Wanting to be somewhere else, Nick wisely started to run away. As he looked for an opening, FemiNazi tripped him up. The psycho villain pointed a pair of machine pistols at his chest, and—

Schling!

Samurai Lou's mystical katana cut through both machine pistols with ease. FemiNazi eyed the Eurasian hero with disbelief as he then punched her in the temple. The blow sent her to the sand, barely conscious. The samurai slapped some sand out of his traditional-style red-and-blue armor as he looked around.

"We have to destroy the lamp!" Samurai Lou yelled with a thick Japanese accent.

"Lamp? What lamp?!" Nick yelped with confusion.

Before the hero could reply, Samurai Lou's eyes widened. He then shoved Nick aside and one-handedly parried eight expertly-thrown daggers. Four Death Grin ninjas moved in for the kill. They wore matching black garb with metal (grinning) masks over their faces. They readied more daggers as Samurai Lou rushed in to protect Nick. As they went at it, Nick suddenly remembered last night and the magic lamp. Looking around, he spotted it in a dead villain's hands—a mere ten feet away.

Samurai Lou gutted one masked ninja, beheaded a second, and slashed yet a third across the belly. But the fourth one threw black acid powder into Samurai Lou's face. Blinded, the samurai stifled a scream as the substance melted through his skin. The hero stubbornly swung at the last ninja, who deftly avoided Lou's blade (twice more) before jamming a pair of daggers into the hero's throat.

The ninja watched Samurai Lou die and then ominously turned toward Nick.

"Oh shit!" Nick exclaimed as he turned and ran for the lamp.

That's when he saw FemiNazi stumble to her feet with a determined scowl. Holstered across her back was a high-tech shotgun. Even though she was seeing double, the villainess couldn't miss at this range. She fired on Nick at full-auto. Behind him, the lone Death Grin ninja threw a fan-like array of daggers with his right hand.

Neither killer should've missed the chubby sophomore at that range. Nick closed his eyes and covered his face with a whimper. During the futile act, FemiNazi's gunfire and the ninja's daggers whizzed past him. FemiNazi gasped as two daggers found her chest.

The ninja flew backwards with a trio of gaping holes in his chest. Unharmed, Nick opened his eyes a few seconds later.

Hope sprouted across his face as he rushed toward the lamp and picked it up. Before Nick could ponder on how to destroy it, Brik landed nearby. In his crimson-hued costume and cape, the villain made pro bodybuilders look small.

"Give me the lamp," scowled the villain.

"How about a punch instead?" asked a third voice. Brik turned around just in time to get clocked in the jaw. The shockwave sent Nick (and anyone else in the vicinity) flying. Clad in his own blue-and-white caped costume, ArgoKnight was slightly smaller than Brik. As the two super-strong bad-asses threw down, Nick knew that Brik would win.

ArgoKnight was the most powerful super hero in this comic's universe. Brik was his main nemesis—the only villain who outmuscled him. In the comics, whenever there was a straight-up fistfight between the two, Brik always won. It usually required teamwork and luck to bring the evil bastard to justice.

Right now, they traded blows so fast that Nick's eyes couldn't follow them all. Then Brik knocked ArgoKnight into the sky. Massaging his right fist, the villain turned on Nick and paused for an aching moment. Brik worked his jaw for a few more seconds and then spat out a bloodied tooth.

"I'll take that," Brik threatened.

"What good is it to you?" Nick asked as he slowly backed away. "I've used up the wishes!"

"Power," Brik replied as he snatched the lamp. "You freed a djinn. If I kill you in the presence of the lamp, you'll take his place. Which will . . ."

". . . recharge the lamp?" Nick quivered.

"Glad you can keep up, kid," Brik mocked as he grabbed nick by the throat. "I think we'll get along just fine."

With ease, the villain lifted Nick off his feet until they were at eye level.

"Then I'll get three wishes for myself," ranted the villain. "And I won't wish for comic book characters, Budweiser oceans, or to be the luckiest man alive. I'll wish for what matters, boy. Power!"

Before Nick could beg for his life, Brik snapped his neck like a potato chip.

A half-second later, ArgoKnight slammed into Brik from above and rained thousands of punches upon him in the space of five seconds. A final overhand right from ArgoKnight put the murderous villain down with a shattered jaw and four more missing teeth.

Bruised and exhausted, the costumed champion looked over his shoulder and watched the last of his fellow heroes fall. Twenty super villains moved toward the lamp, all eager to be the one who claimed its wishes.

Only ArgoKnight stood in their way.

The caped hero knew that others would come for the lamp—both good and evil. Like everyone else, he had rushed through the night to get here. Right now, he was humanity's last hope. How he knew about Nick, the djinn, or the lamp didn't matter. What did was that he returned things back to normal. If not, humanity would be threatened by countless world-ending threats. Even with real super heroes around, ArgoKnight knew that they couldn't stop them all—not in the real world.

And there was that beer ocean thing . . .

ArgoKnight slapped his gloved hands together with more force than a Category 5 hurricane. The resulting shockwave hurled the remaining villains backwards. Half-buried by sand, the villains were out of the fight. The hero picked up the lamp and rubbed it three times.

Nick's soul appeared next to his corpse, in the same clothes he died in. Visibly shaken, the newly-minted djinn looked down at his corpse and yelled a girlish scream.

"Am I dead?!" Nick asked.

"Yes," ArgoKnight urgently replied. "You are the djinn now. I have three wishes. Grant them so I can save the day."

Nick nodded and then turned to face the ocean.

"I can't believe I turned the oceans of the world into Budweiser!"

"Me neither," ArgoKnight replied straight-faced. "What's wrong with Guinness?"

For a moment, the fictional hero and Nick shared a grin. Then ArgoKnight was all-business again.

"My first wish is that all three of your wishes are completely reversed—after my third wish. Second, I wish that all magic lamps on this world cease to be—after my third wish. And third, I—uggh!"

A glowing red spear savagely exited through ArgoKnight's stomach.

PsiSpear grinned as his intangible body turned corporeal. Essentially a living thought, the villain twisted his psychic fighting spear to worsen the damage. Blood came out of ArgoKnight's mouth as he dropped the lamp and fell to his knees. The skinny villain whipped his psychic weapon free and dispelled it with a whim. ArgoKnight's blood sprayed in all directions, including the villain's gray-and-black uniform.

"No third wishes for you," PsiSpear spat as he stepped over the dying hero and moved to pick up the lamp with his free hand.

ArgoKnight gasped his third wish—something so barely audible that only Nick could hear it—but it was enough. With a smile, Nick granted it.

* * *

Nick jumped awake under the early dawn light. He looked around and saw only his liquor bottle, the dried vomit, and the beautiful blue-green waters of the Atlantic. He pulled the panties off his head and tossed them aside.

"What a gawdawful dream," Nick yawned with a relieved smile.

The hungover sophomore sipped the last of the sun-warmed whiskey. Once it was gone, he tossed the bottle and rose to his feet. A cool morning breeze hit him as he stepped over the vomit and stumbled for the beach house to take a long and meaningful piss.

Overhead, ArgoKnight smiled down at Nick and flew away toward the rising sun.

CONSIDER IT DONE

Detective Lou Sho stepped into the glitzy lobby of the massive *Gidara Conglomerates Tower*. He was here to solve an intriguing crime. Early this afternoon, multiple stun pulse generators went off through the building, enough to stun everyone inside the massive skyscraper. According to the preliminary claims, the 4,087 people in the building were rendered unconscious for 15 minutes. Most of the victims suffered bumps and bruises, with a few dozen sent to the hospital for more serious injuries. This appeared to have been some kind of raid with a yet unknown objective. The preliminary head count suggested that no one had been abducted. The building's bank (and its vault) were untouched. While some people were gunned down prior to the incident, they weren't worth this much effort.

Sho looked around. The only visible traces of the crime were a few long-dried coffee spills and some dropped papers. The rest of the space was taken up by hovering evidence drones and cops. He did notice the odd smell of ozone in the air—a result of the SPGs. Normally used for riot control, Sho figured that seven properly spaced units could take out the building. They could've dropped everyone for up to an hour.

Instead, the killers opted for a quarter-hour—minimizing their chances of being interrupted. Once they did their thing, the clever bastards either fled the scene or ditched their gear and blended in with the stunned victims. Whatever the plan was, they were done before the first responders bypassed the security lockdown, some twenty minutes later.

One of Frank Upiah's uniformed security goons arrived at the scene. Sho sized up the huge guard's impeccable physique, which implied cyberware. From what he knew, most of Upiah's head crushers were cyborgs. They packed black market tech and were loyal to the same drug cartel that Mr. Upiah allegedly laundered money for.

Unimpressed, Sho saw Upiah for what he was: a high-level figurehead trying to play honest citizen. While the banker was generous with his creds and clout, everyone knew he was dirty. No one could prove it because the cartel paid so many people to look the other way—including Sho. Any cop not on the take ended up leaving the force or dying in the line of duty.

Such was the life of a civil servant.

The Eurasian detective put a stick of caff gum in his mouth and returned to work. He questioned the CSI techs and sized up the killers' most likely path of progression. After being on the scene for an hour, the veteran detective was still wondering what the hell the intruders' objective had been. The more he learned, the less sense it made.

Eight military-grade stun pulse generators were found (thus far)—probably stolen. The company techs had yet to find any sign of systems sabotage or information hack, which didn't surprise Sho. Data thefts were done with far more discretion by pros who weren't crazy enough to pull this stunt on cartel turf.

A pair of techs then informed Sho that the security room was deemed safe to enter. Unlike the rest of the building, the ovular room had been trashed—first by the killers than by the fire department. Prior to the lockdown, the killers breached this room and opened fire. The bodies of four uniformed cyborgs were on the floor, all riddled with small arms fire. All of them were leaking blood and damaged cyber components. Even with their augmented reflexes, none of them managed to draw their weapons.

This was where the security lockdown had been triggered. Rather than hack the systems, the killers merely took over the controls. They set it off just before triggering the SPGs. Since the security room was shielded against stun pulses, it made the perfect bunker. Once everyone else dropped, they unlocked anything they wanted. On the way out, they left timed incendiary charges. When they went off, the security feeds were charred.

Moving through the carnage, Sho was so distracted that he almost stepped onto the corpse of the fifth victim. Unlike the others, this one was a pregnant woman, just within her first trimester. Her half-charred badge identified her as IT. There were two exit wounds in her forehead, which suggested she had been killed execution-style.

Sho ignored a tech's assertion that a large team did this.

Large teams made mistakes. Granted, this was a 130-story building. That meant a lot of ground to cover, which would make a large team logical. The detective saw it another way. A small, elite group went in with extensive inside knowledge of the building and months of prep. They could move faster and leave fewer traces in their wake.

The balls of it all amazed the detective, as did the fact that Upiah survived all of this—

"Detective?"

Sho turned toward one of the techs. Like the others, he wore the black-and-white SFPD forensic scrubs, utility harness, and tox mask.

"Yeah?"

"Mr. Upiah wants to see you," said the tech.

The tech's deferential tone almost implied that he was taking cartel cash as well. That wouldn't have surprised Sho. Whoever controlled the evidence controlled the case. Sho nodded and headed for the elevator, certain that he was missing something. If Upiah concealed or erased the evidence, this case would be impossible to solve.

The elevator let off on the 129th floor, outside of Upiah's private office. Sho patiently allowed himself to get scanned and disarmed by Upiah's personal security. Then eight guards escorted him into the financier's presence. Sho was 190 pounds of lean muscle in a decent suit. Too honest to spend his monthly bribes on anything but charity, he gave Frank Upiah a polite nod.

Handshakes were as extinct as cursive and decent music. Yet, the bear of a money launderer extended his right hand and had a firm grip. In his late 50's, Upiah had twenty years on Sho and outweighed the cop by over 100 pounds. His impeccably-tailored suit was worth more than the detective's car.

"I understand that you called for me, Mr. Upiah?" Sho asked with a forced smile.

"That I did," Upiah replied with a cultured New England accent and deep voice. "I've been told that you were placed in charge of this investigation?"

"That's correct, sir."

"Good," Upiah nodded with an insincere smile. "I need it closed within the hour."

Sho blinked.

"Excuse me, sir?"

"The perpetrators were a team of domestic terrorists, detective," explained the criminal. "Suspects and evidence will be provided. SWAT's en route as we speak. You'll handle the arrests."

The money launderer then leaned in close enough to smell Sho's mint-flavored caff gum.

"And if it's not too much trouble, detective, do kill them all. I'm sure they'll resist arrest."

Sho thought of the pregnant woman and her unborn child, pleased he didn't have any family of his own. Cops had two vulnerabilities: greed and family. The detective didn't care about being a clean cop—just a good one. He liked solving crimes and putting bad people in jail or the morgue. Of seeing some kind of justice done in these darkened times.

He frowned at the thought of slaughtering a group of patsies. Granted, Upiah's "suspects" probably deserved a date with the Reaper. Yet he had busted enough domestic terrorist types to doubt they had anything to do with this criminal masterpiece.

Sho wanted them—bad.

The detective continued to ponder the request while Upiah's bodyguards regarded him with a quiet menace. The few cops and techs in the massive office looked on like frightened woodland animals. Sho slipped his hands into his pockets and stared Upiah in the eye.

"No."

Upiah blinked with surprise at the detective's rude reply.

"Excuse me?" asked the money launderer.

"Someone attacked your building, Mr. Upiah," replied the detective. "The sophistication was far beyond some easy-to-catch domestic terrorists. Your 'clients' should want the people who did this, in case this happens again somewhere else. So point them out. Then we'll serve and protect."

Upiah's face and posture both tensed up.

"Detective, you're way out of line. I don't care—"

"That's what makes no sense, Mr. Upiah. You should care," Sho asserted. "If I had this egg on my face, I'd be out for blood and scared for my life at the same time. Someone pulled this off on your watch, Mr. Upiah. Five dead, millions in damage, and you're treating this like a mild setback? With your company stock in such a slump . . ."

Sho paused as his quick mind did the life-saving math.

Then he noticed dried pools of blood behind Upiah's desk. No one told him about that. If everyone in the building had been stunned, without disrupting the elevators, it would've been easy to cap Upiah. Even if this office was shielded and Upiah made it to some kind of panic room, the killers would've accounted for that.

Sho glanced over at the blood again. It was thick enough to be arterial. His gut told him that it belonged to Frank Upiah. Yet here stood the money laundering CEO, without a scratch on him.

"Forgive my reaction, sir," Sho sighed with mock regret. "I'm simply doing what's best for the company."

Upiah's surprised frown was mimicked by everyone else in the room.

"Might I offer a more effective solution?"

Upiah folded his arms.

"Go ahead, detective."

"An anonymous tip would make more sense," Sho replied. "Enough for search warrants but not too much—or everyone'll smell a cover-up. We'll follow the evidence. After a week or two, we'll find these murderous sons of bitches."

The money launderer thoughtfully pursed his lips.

"Then what?"

"SWAT goes in and you have your bloodbath," urged the detective. "Make it look realistic or the net bloggers will get too interested in your domestic terrorists."

Sho gave the cyborg to his left a friendly smile, surprised that no one else had figured it out yet . . . or maybe they had. Normally, firing a CEO involved meetings, bribes, lawsuits, a few dozen murders, and some vid blather. The cartel had a better idea. They killed the "outgoing" CEO and inserted a surgically-altered imposter.

"Thanks for the advice, Detective," said Upiah. "I'll be sure to voice my praises to your lieutenant. There might even be a promotion for you."

"No need, sir," Sho replied as he offered his hand. "I'm more of a street guy."

The imposter shook Sho's hand and then frowned when the cop didn't let go.

"But if you could do one last thing for me, that'd be great."

"Name it, detective," the fake Upiah replied without moving.

"Whoever killed that pregnant lady, on the first floor, please donate his vital organs to charity by week's end," Sho kindly demanded. "Do that and I'll personally close this case by-the-book. Sir."

The money launderer read Sho's knowing eyes and realized that the detective had indeed figured this out. Instead of asking for more money or threatening to go to the press, he wanted street justice. His superiors could either erase a member of the cartel's best kill team or a decorated detective, whose cooperation could efficiently close this case.

"Consider it done," vowed the new CEO.

ONE LAST QUEST

Whatever used to be blocking the cave had been blasted down. Shattered pieces of glass, rock, and metal were scattered across the opening. A detachment of Dastrayan knights was supposed to guard it 24/7, which they did . . . until someone expertly chopped them up. Grouped en masse, they must've valiantly died. I dismounted from my jittery roan and eyed the mountain pass.

"The Gate has been breached!" Brother Minsla pointed with a gnarled old index finger.

I bit my sarcastic tongue as I spared the monk an evil glance. The old man had personally led us up here, failing health and all. That earned him a pass. Perched on a mule, Minsla's face was twisted with outrage at such an apparent sacrilege.

I should've known better than to hope that this way home wouldn't be yet another dud.

At the heart of the cave was the Gate of Twisted Paths. A doorway between realms, it was supposed to get our sorry hides back home. I turned to Gant and Hiddows, pissed at how everything had gone so wrong this time.

It all began with a subway ride on a rainy Tuesday morning. I'll never forget how the skyline went from Brooklyn and then out through a low waterfall. Still moving at significant speed, the landing was rough. We now in the world of Drakrim (in the elven nation). A group of elven traders came across us and tried to save anyone not instantly crushed in the crash.

Of the fifty-two passengers, eighteen survived.

The elves took us to their king, who graciously offered permanent refuge within their boring, safe lands. Half of us stayed, content by the hassle-free beauty of the elven realm. But I wasn't satisfied with this world. I was an over-educated thug from Queens. I liked toothpaste and stolen cars. Ice cubes and cable. It's funny what you miss when you're not on Earth anymore. This world was the shitty equivalent of the Dark Ages: only with magic, monsters, asshole gods, and way too much despair for my taste.

The elves schooled us, supplied us, and wished us luck. We nine stuck together, fought for our lives, and died off over our six-year quest. We bounced from one dead-end way home to another. Most were bullshit. A few had been destroyed or came with too many strings attached.

Just getting permission to use the Gate of Twisted Paths required us to save a young king's life and stop a rebellion. That miracle took five weeks of hard fighting and some incredibly stupid risk-taking. Yet the cause was just and when the smoke cleared we were living legends. I turned down a betrothal to the king's busty, jailbait sister for the best chance to get home to cheese fries and PlayStation.

And now this . . .

Most holy men were priests who favored a god or two. As a monk, Minsla worshipped all of 'em—even the dark ones. He figured they all had their purpose in this world. Still on his mule, the monk bowed his head and uttered a prayer to Origul, Goddess of Death, to shepherd the fallen knights to their version of Valhalla.

"What now?" Hiddows asked.

The beefy stamp collector had turned into a large, barrel-chested badass with a massive war hammer slung over his right shoulder. Back home, he was a geekus maximus working out of a Best Buy with no chance of losing his virginity without paid help. But here, Hiddows had a flair for navigating us through this roleplayer's wet dream. The more of this world he saw, the more he wanted to stay.

"We go in," Gant replied.

A single mother of two, she had been the driving force for us to get home since minute one. Slim and mean, we followed her lead. Back home, she was a corporate manager type who used to bow hunt with her uncle as a kid. Here, she could put an arrow through a door lock at fifty yards.

They both dismounted their horses and followed me.

"Should we wait for you, Lord Omar?" Minsla asked.

My black ass was so not used to the title and never would be.

"If we're not back in an hour, leave our horses and return home," I replied, annoyed that I was turning my back on land, titles, busty jailbait, and a few chests of gold . . . a small "thank-you" for saving a kingdom from the Zultyrim.

If there was one thing about being here that I enjoyed, it was killing Zultyrim. It's like the gods got together and created a race of pure assholes just to fuck with the rest of us. I had yet to meet one Zultyrim worth a damn. They were universally hated because they were xenophobic bigots who loved to fight. They were so filled with hatred that they even stand each other. Only the "joy" of killing everyone else kept their empire together. Thus began their centuries-long crusade to take over the world. Kingdom-by-kingdom, the world fell to them with the survivors forced to endure hopeless slavery.

Divided by old animosities and feuds, none of the remaining kingdoms would band together. Even if they did, I wouldn't bet on them to win (even the elves). The Zultyrim—bastards that they were—knew how to wage war. They had the best knights, commanders, and combat mystics in the world. Yeah, they'd win someday.

But that wasn't my problem. Getting home was.

"Gods be with you," Minsla uttered, ending his prayer over the fallen knights.

Gant muttered something about what the gods could go do with themselves. As it turned out, we were stranded on this world because of some silly divine wager. There was a warlord named Jovyr Miet who liked looting temples and raping priestesses. Something of a lunatic, he had acquired some ancient artifact—an amulet—that made him un-killable by anyone born of Drakrim.

Then, one day, we just "happened" to wander into his path. Thirty of them. Three of us. The fight was quick and dirty. Hiddows and I slaughtered Jovyr's entourage. Gant put an arrow through Jovyr's mouth while he was bragging at how un-killable he was. Hiddows—who was a walking shit-magnet—kept the amulet, for luck. That was about four years ago. A few months after that encounter, an oracle revealed to us that we had been brought here to kill Jovyr. Our destinies fulfilled, the gods had no further interest in us.

Needless to say, we hated the fuckers.

"You two should turn back," Gant said without a hint of guilt-trip in her hazel eyes.

She had become the most awesome woman I ever knew. Strong, compassionate, and honest, we'd follow her into Hell and burn the fucker down because she'd find a way for us to do it. Still, even she had to admit that this was a fucking trap. Just as I was about to bring that up—

"I will stick around," Hiddows stated as he hefted *GodPounder* in his mailed right hand. "After I see you two through that Gate."

Figured he'd say that, which was why I never brought it up. As filthy as this world was, the adventure bug had gotten into his blood. Gant gave him a sad, understanding smile. Hiddows held out his left hand, palm-down.

"One last quest," Hiddows grinned.

The phrase was our slogan. We uttered it every time we had a chance to leave this fucking world.

"One last quest," Gant smiled as she slapped her right hand on Hiddows'.

"Fuckin' better be," I muttered as I slapped my right hand over theirs.

We shared a moment. Then we readied our weapons.

"Usual formation?" I asked.

Gant nodded.

She liked me taking point. We were about the same height, which made it easier for her to shoot arrows past my head in a pinch. Hiddows was covered in defensive runes, protected by the amulet, and had a verified god killing weapon. Covering our backs was his specialty. Gant and I didn't even bother checking our six o'clocks anymore.

Me? I liked to rhyme. Funny thing about singing on this world is that if you're willing to risk your soul, it's possible to cut loose with a verse and turn it into a spell. A group of bards developed the technique and one of them taught it to me. While they used limericks, I liked rap. Do it right and the same verse could be used for combat magic, healing magic, illusions, or whatever else. But you have to keep your focus and balance. If your focus is off, the verse is just words. If your balance is off, then spell casting could make you dead real quick.

I called my stuff "Verse Magic." Not as powerful as the traditional styles of magic, it was easy to learn and way more versatile. With my short swords out, I started spitting the lyrics *It Ain't A Crime* by House of Pain. As I rapped, I walked over to the knights and took in the scene. A number of simple facts immediately caught my attention. The knights' blades weren't drawn, which meant they didn't (or couldn't) fight back. Their horses were gone without a single one of them falling. Each knight died from behind—either back stabbed or with a slit throat. No spent arrows or discarded weapons were found. None of that followed. Knights of Dastraya were hard-core kickers of ass, some of whom dabbled with spell casting (like me). Beating them—unscathed—was next to impossible.

Halfway through the first refrain, the divination spell kicked in.

No one else died here. There was plenty of blood on the ground . . . all of it theirs.

I couldn't sense any bad guys, which didn't mean shit. Enough mystics (working in tandem) could use cloaking magic and stealth cover a small army. Still, residual magic blanketed the valley... temporal magic. Someone powerful had slammed a massive time freeze over these poor bastards.

Anyone in its path would freeze in time, allowing anyone else to walk up and kill them with ease. The spell was high-end, Zultyrim in nature, and too powerful to cloak. Even though the spell expired, someone was keeping the energies on a mystical standby—to use on us. I could feel the energies surge. I needed the caster's name and the Verse gave it to me. His name was Yizelleck.

I stopped in mid-verse and turned to Gant.

"What do you see?" Gant asked, her gorgon bone bow clutched in her delicate left hand. The bones were hand-glued from a dead gorgon and assembled like a macabre jigsaw puzzle. Once per day, it would hit anyone she named, whether she could see him or not.

"A Zultyrim named Yizelleck," I simply replied, with a nod to my nine o'clock.

Gant smirked and then whispered the man's name into her bow. It hummed as she deftly notched a barbed arrow and sent it streaking out of the canyon. Right as it disappeared from view, we could hear a male half-scream. Had he not turned to stone, he might've finished the sound.

"You should've taken the lordship," Hiddows frowned, reading my face.

Instead of telling him which side of my ass to kiss, I cut loose with *Rhymes Galore*.

"Shit!" Gant muttered, knowing that I only went with Busta Rhymes when a heavy fight was brewing. The pace put me in an amped up mood and best of all—it was short. Only, instead of combat magic, I needed to hijack that temporal spell.

Hiddows and Gant stood back-to-back and watched mine.

I built up the spell with each verse, feeding it with my soul. The longer it went, the more of me it would take. Too much at one time would kill me (or worse). As I rapped, Minsla closed his eyes and began to pray. While I only had weak-assed Verse magic, he could ask the gods for divine aid. If he asked the right deity at the right time, the old priest could (literally) pull a miracle out of thin air.

Near the end of *Rhymes Galore,* Minsla wailed in agony and fell off his mule.

The dead priest hit the ground with a crossbow bolt in his back. Just like that, the air stunk of magic as Zultyrim combat mystics jumped out of the ground and canyon walls. There must've been a hundred of them (at least) without a mere soldier in the mix. Another twenty or so rushed out of the entrance. They wielded a variety of mystical weapons, talismans, and shit I couldn't recognize. Bare-chested and covered with glyphic tattoos, they look pretty cocky.

"No wonder the knights died so easy," Gant muttered.

One of the fuckers stepped forward. Big and scary-looking, he wielded a wicked-looking scimitar and gave us a sneer.

"Surrender! Or we'll—*aaacckkk!*"

Gant interrupted his threat with an arrow to the balls. Poor guy dropped to his knees and died a statue (with an arrow through his nuts). He would've looked great in my backyard. Anyway, the rest of his cohorts shouted their war cries. In a few more seconds, they'd attack. Some had weapons. Others came at us barehanded. A few were chanting their attack spells, waiting for Yizelleck to lay out his spell.

Hah! They didn't know he was dead.

The whole time, I kept versing.

"What's the plan?" Hiddows asked, more worried about us than himself.

I abruptly stopped rapping and grinned as time stopped around us. In this entire valley, nothing moved up us and our mounts.

"Nice spell," Gant said, lowering her bow.

"More like a spelljacking," I admitted.

"How long's it gonna last?" she asked.

"Ten minutes or—*uurrkkk!*," I managed, before the spell drain suddenly hit. Being a dabbler, heavyweight magicks took a wicked toll on me. The world spun as I dropped to one knee.

"Do we run away or see if the Gate's in one piece?" Gant asked.

"Assume the Gate's trashed or cursed," Hiddows muttered before smashing a nearby Zultyrim in the face with his hammer—with no apparent effect. Frozen in time, the mystic didn't even budge. Of course, once the spell ended, his skull would explode.

"We need to get lost," Gant said as she slung her bow across her back.

"Grab a talker," I muttered as Hiddows helped me up with his free hand. "We can torture some answers out of him later."

"What about the rest of them?" Gant asked as she and Hiddows helped me onto my saddle.

I grabbed the reins and shook off the delirium as best I could. It would pass in an hour or two.

"Can we kill them all?" Hiddows asked with a grin and a vial of swirling white liquid.

"Is that a Hell Vial?" I groaned, amazed he was stupid enough to lug that shit anywhere near me.

"My last one," grinned the muscular killing machine. "Should I use it?"

A product of ancient alchemical warfare, this shit could cook a mid-sized city. Once he popped the cork and shattered the vial, everyone in this bowl-shaped valley would enjoy something biblical.

"Stop asking dumb questions and grab that talker," Gant grinned as she mounted her mare.

Hiddows looked amused as he popped the cork, shattered the vial, and rushed over to his stallion. Frozen in time, the contents looked harmless enough. They wouldn't be in about ten minutes.

"What about that talker?" I reminded them (again).

"Dude, they're Zultyrim," he laughed. "Their diabolical plan's to kill us. Always will be."

"See your point," I admitted.

"I would like to know who told them we'd be here," Gant scowled with a glance at poor Minsla. "Someone sold us out."

While the old man didn't deserve to be left here, he'd approve of the way we avenged him.

"Fine," I sighed. "As long as we torture the right someone."

"Works for me," Hiddows nodded.

With that, we rode for our lives. We were out of the valley a full minute-plus before time resumed its natural flow. Intense flames and girly-man screams roared from behind us. We didn't bother to stop and admire our handiwork. We won. They lost. All that mattered was the next quest and hoping that the next get-home-quick scheme was gonna work.

I did know one thing for certain: if I made it back home, I'd truly miss this shit.

THE TROJAN POX

I made a living playing cards (a skill I picked up in the joint). Aside from solving crimes and killing people, it was about my only real talent. My fellow back-alley gamblers accepted me into their ranks without prejudice. We misfits were like family. One of them, Lia Blake, came to me with a problem yesterday. While gambling was her hobby, her mainstay was making fake IDs. Lia told me that she had whipped up a batch of passports for some scary guys. She was meeting them to get paid and asked me to tag along—in case they had other ideas. Poor gal told me the when and where. I turned her down because I was too chickenshit to risk another felony conviction. Frustrated, Lia cussed me out and left.

Then I got a case of conscience and followed her some ten minutes later.

I passed the parking lot where the deal was going to go down and headed there on foot. The ex-cop in me was prepared enough to bring a street-bought gun. Three fuckers drove up on Lia and gunned her down. Instead of racing off, they got out and started loading her body.

That's when I got involved. I fed two of them a clip's worth of hollow points. The third one got away with the passports. Since Lia was too dead to save, I fled the scene before the cops showed. That's when I reached out to Connie, my old partner.

Were it not for the fact that she was happily married (and knew better than to date a loser like me) I would've proposed to her years ago, back when we were mere beat cops. While Connie would never admit it, I could see it in her eyes at times. She cared for me. It was the only reason she answered my call. Thank God she did.

Any other sane cop would've let me sink. After my wife died, I married a needle and slowly disintegrated. Connie was too distracted to notice, until I.A. busted me for drug use and dealing on the side (to support my habit). I just couldn't leave the heroin alone. Even in prison, I was a junkie. I'd have punched my own ticket if Connie hadn't been waiting when I made parole. Out of guilt and loyalty, she half-dragged me into rehab and got me straightened out.

These days, Connie had earned her detective shield and was working Homicide. I asked her to look into Lia's case. She called in some favors and came back with some interesting prelim. The two dead guys turned out to be decorated ex-Marines who had pulled multiple tours in Iraq. Both men were already under FBI surveillance for their anti-government tendencies. Who were they killing for? The cops had no idea—yet.

I wanted their boss because Lia was a friend. That's why I went to her trailer-sized storage locker/office and poked around. There was a discarded passport photo with a name scribbled under it: V.Z. Trefstein. I found him on Google and looked through his bio on my phone.

Vincent Zacharias Trefstein was an Army bio-warfare chemist who quit and became an outspoken anti-war advocate. His grassroots organization held some protests with little success beyond the occasional bits of media coverage. One recent article suggested that Trefstein had given up the cause and left the spotlight.

I couldn't find anything else of value and stepped outside to call Connie in. Only, two of Trefstein's goons were waiting for me outside. One of them shot the fuck out of my car as I hopped in and fled the scene. The other one got in my way, which was how his skull ended up through my windshield.

As I raced away, trying to think of my next move, the guy in my windshield regained consciousness. Poor fucker almost made me crash. I pulled into a dark alley and tended to his injuries with a crowbar. He mumbled something about a "Trojan Pox" and how Congress would get what it deserved.

I might've learned about the rest of the conspiracy if the bastard hadn't chosen that particular moment to die. Fuck. I searched his body and found a photo for Maria (Connie's only child) in his pocket, with her school's name scribbled on the back. I pulled the corpse off my car and called Connie. She didn't pick up.

So I muffled my voice, called 9-1-1, and threw out an anonymous kidnapping tip. I left out the Trojan Pox reference because dispatch wouldn't take me seriously— not without ironclad proof. That's why I stupidly raced over to the school with a bloody hole in my windshield and a stolen gun in my belt. I must've been begging to get my ass thrown back inside. Then I remembered what Lia looked like on the ground. There was no way I'd let them whack Connie's kid.

I showed up at the ass-end of a shootout. From the look of things, a patrol car had gotten to the school first. The two dead cops were inside, both chewed up by assault weapons before crashing into a tree. Maria was nowhere in sight and somehow three bad guys got left behind.

From the cover of a few parked cars, the pricks traded gunfire with Connie and an older guy in a cheap suit (I guessed her current partner). She must've gotten the 9-1-1 call and rushed over to get her kid. The two detectives were pinned down behind their unmarked car. Connie dropped one of the kidnappers before she ran out of ammo. Then her partner took one to the skull. The other two moved in for the kill.

Being all civic-minded, I pinned the closest rat bastard between my front bumper and the side of a parked pickup truck (at about fifty miles an hour). Had my airbag not deployed, I'd have been able to shoot his partner. As the last guy leisurely walked up to me and aimed for a skull shot, Connie capped him with her partner's piece. Then she helped me out of my wrecked car.

Almost on cue, her cell phone rang. Maria was on the other end. She sobbingly told her mom to toss our cell phones and to bring me to 4319 Pursner Street—alone and right now—or she'd end up with a slit throat. Connie and I argued over what to do next. Me? I thought it was a stupid not to call in SWAT but she figured that they had ears in the department. Judging from the way the bad guys were onto us, I had to agree.

So we commandeered a car and surrendered. Trefstein's guys frisked us, split us up, and sat me down. Only then did the big man show up. He was dressed in a tux, as were half of his guys. When I asked Trefstein about the Trojan Pox, he gleefully filled in the blanks.

The Trefsteins were a military family, tracing their wartime roots to the Spanish-American War. His son was a Marine who took some shrapnel to the chest during an ambush in Afghanistan. His comrades went into hostile fire and pulled him out. They patched him up, saved his life, and sent him home. He should've lived. Instead, the young soldier died from some preventable infection in a "third-rate" veteran's hospital.

Trefstein blamed Congress for the conditions of that hospital and so many other failings. They were willing to waste taxpayer dollars on wars, yet so little on the veterans who fought and died in them. Nearing the end of his own military service, Trefstein heard about the Trojan Pox and swapped out a vial with a placebo.

The military accidentally discovered Trojan Pox after 9/11. The stuff equated to a fast-acting case of smallpox, which moved through one's system like shit through a goose. About 97% contagious, anyone who got it had an hour to live. The weird thing was that infected folks felt just fine . . . until about fifty minutes after exposure. Then the symptoms would hit both abruptly and painfully, followed by certain death. To date, the Army hadn't yet come up with either a suitable vaccine or antidote.

Trefstein found his grassroots organization as a cover to embezzle money (to fund this scheme), recruit like-minded zealots, and achieve a bit of sympathetic publicity. That last part was necessary. For, while his team was infecting Congress with the Pox, Trefstein would be at a scheduled press conference—confessing his scheme on national TV. He predicted that by the time the authorities quarantined the area, the Pox would be contained and both Houses of Congress would be decimated.

It was a crazy plan and full of holes . . . but it just might've worked.

Both Houses were in session. His people had managed to gain media access to Capitol Hill. If they made it through without detection, they could infect themselves and then guide the path of the Pox. Trefstein hoped to take out so many members of Congress that the institution would have to be re-populated from scratch—hopefully by less corrupt motherfuckers. Trefstein would plead guilty and end up in prison for life a big man.

From behind bars, the peace advocate would've pressed for the American people to scrap the current two-party system and replace it with something more representative and remotely useful. Such a scheme could've caused chaos, another civil war, true political reform, and/or human extinction.

Well, the asshole made three massive mistakes.

First, Trefstein figured that Connie would talk—or watch her daughter and me die. As they mashed my left eye shut with repeated punches, Trefstein had only one guard with him (another mistake). The second that guard took his eyes off Connie, she crushed his windpipe. The only reason Trefstein made it out of the room was that I used the distraction to snatch a gun. I then opened fire.

That was his third (and worse) mistake: not tying me up.

I mean really? They had this big-time master scheme but never equipped themselves to deal with prisoners? Rope, handcuffs, or even a bullet through the knee would've made the difference. They figured I wouldn't move with two hostages on the other side of the glass (and they were right). The sadistic assholes relished the idea of me sitting there, taking a beating.

Well, they didn't see Connie get the upper hand. Through one good eye, I did. That's when I did my thing. The rest was a violent blur. When it was over, I was in a lot of fucking pain with two bullets in my gut. There was one live baddie left in the room. He had a clear vial of Pox in his right hand and an empty Beretta in the other. Scared and sweaty, he ordered me to drop my piece.

I glanced over at Connie, who shoved Maria to the floor. Trefstein was already gone. The minion started to repeat his threat when I fed my last four rounds into him. Connie popped up just in time to see the vial on the floor. My ex-partner gave me a sad look and then wisely snatched up her kid and ran for the stairs.

Connie will tell them why we ended up in this abandoned basement/meth lab; a staging area for (what would've been) one of the worst terrorist acts in American history. What a story she'd have to tell. Wishing for a hit of morphine, there was nothing left for me to do but die.

INALIENABLE RIGHTS

Gail Hines leaned against the polished bar of
Chockney's Pub, drawn in by the TV evening news
footage to her left and the heated chatter along the
crowded bar. A cute, jeans-wearing blonde in her early
20's, the waitress fingered a silver cross worn on a
matching chain around her tight-fitting *Chockney's* t-
shirt. Being raised a moderate Roman Catholic, Gail
found this current controversy somewhat disturbing. It
was all centered on the latest press conference given by
Nathan Whilte, an independent candidate running for
President.

Handsome, suave, and articulate, the Senator had
decided to run for the White House. His message was
straightforward, creative, and realistic. The media and
the public adored him: especially compared to his rival
candidates and their tired, over-used platforms. Gail
wasn't the least bit surprised that Whilte had won both
the Iowa Caucus and the New Hampshire Primary.
According the polls, he had a double-digit lead on any of
his other five opponents. He had sufficient grassroots
funding and plenty of friends in high places. Barring a
scandal, Whilte was a shoe-in for President.

Then that very scandal reared its ugly head. During
an interview on *Sixty Minutes*, some whacko priest
stormed onto the stage and splashed holy water on
Whilte's face. As the priest was wrestled to the ground
by Whilte's Secret Service detail, the presidential front-
runner reverted to his true form.

The Senator's Caucasian features turned crimson.
His hazel eyes became all-black and larger. Curved
black horns rose from his forehead. Six-inch claws slid
out from his fingertips. His perfect nose became a
hideous snout. When it was over, Senator Whilte had

grown a half-foot in height. His musculature expanded enough to rip his expensive blue suit at the seams. Then there were the cloven hooves and the membranous crimson wings which shot out of his back. The holy water burned Whilte like acid, who dropped to his knees with an inhuman roar. That's when someone cut the footage.

Millions of Americans were tuned in that night. Billions of humans were tuned in the following day.

Naturally, Whilte was on the front page of every newspaper on Earth: the demonic presidential front-runner of the most powerful nation in the world. His attacker was identified as Father Julius Gess. Gess had baptized Whilte when he was a baby. Back then, the child's forehead smoked during the ritual pouring of holy water.

Everyone else figured it was a trick of the light or something—but not Gess. When interviewed, the priest explained that he had warned the Vatican, which opted for a "wait-and-see" approach. The priest kept tabs on Nathan Whilte ever since. When Gess saw how well Whilte's campaign was going, he felt compelled to reveal the candidate's true nature to the world.

The media went over Whilte's personal background again. No one could find any prior hint about his demonic nature. The only odd thing in his past involved his parents. During an interview, Whilte intimated that his mother had been attacked and raped by an unknown assailant.

Barely twenty at the time, she ended up in the hospital with bruises and no recollection of her attacker's face. The police investigated the incident but never found the assailant. When she became pregnant, Whilte's mom decided to raise him alone. Dead from lung cancer, his mom wasn't available for comment.

Aside from the details of his conception, the rest of his past was well-documented. The Senator grew up a "normal" kid from Washington State. Whilte entered the Marine Corps at eighteen and fought two tours in Vietnam, earning three Purple Hearts and a Bronze Star. After Vietnam, he went to Notre Dame on the GI Bill and became a mechanical engineer. In time, Whilte started inventing useful consumer gadgets and made a fortune.

He donated generously to charity and even helped start a charitable foundation aimed at promoting racial equality. In time, he got married and adopted three beautiful daughters. There was never a whiff of scandal from him or his family. When he turned forty-nine, Whilte decided to run for a seat in the House of Representatives as a Republican.

Even though he had lost in the primaries, the GOP liked him so much that they asked him to run again in the next election. He politely declined, switched his status to independent and ran for the Senate instead, where he won a close race against a scandal-plagued Democratic incumbent.

His first six-year term had been filled with numerous triumphs and few failures. A truly moderate conservative, Whilte had a knack for picking the right side of any debate. His enemies were few and had grudgingly respected him—up until that night.

Now, Whilte was at the center of a political maelstrom. The candidate was expected to immediately drop out of the race and resign his Senate seat. Instead, Whilte called a news conference the next day. He arrived (in human form) with his wife and daughters at his back. Whilte then politely told everyone that he intended to continue his campaign.

He apologized for not revealing his true nature prior to entering politics. Then Whilte argued that his unique "ethnicity" was his business. He expressed his gratitude to his wife and daughters for keeping his secret. Then he went on to explain why he would continue his campaign. Basically, the nation needed sound leadership, which Whilte felt he could provide. He explained that this wasn't about ego or stubbornness. It was about serving his country, yet again. Whilte felt that the wisdom of the American voter should determine whether or not he got the chance to do that.

Naturally, the religious community was in an uproar. Catholics and Muslims (for once) universally agreed that Whilte shouldn't be President. Were Whilte to win, key religious leaders warned, he would be feared and distrusted throughout the world. More rabble-rousing religious pundits called him the "Anti-Christ." More radical types even called for him to be sent back to Hell in a body bag.

Politically, most of Whilte's supporters distanced themselves. Key donors found themselves divided between his sterling record of public service . . . and his species. His opponents gave open-minded comments. In private, they quietly rejoiced and courted Whilte's donors.

Oddly enough, his support amongst under-30 voters increased. Pollsters had all types of goofy theories to explain this: ranging from a lack of school prayer to there being too many sci-fi geeks out there. Legally, efforts were underway to force him to step down. There was even talk of the case going to the Supreme Court.

One of Gail's half-drunken patrons snagged her attention by claiming that Whilte's candidacy was protected by the Founding Fathers and the Constitution. The guy was born in the United States. He was over 35 years old. Technically, he asserted, a talking goat, born in this country, could run for President if he/she was older than 35—in goat years, of course.

Someone threw popcorn at him for the goat reference. Another (more inebriated) patron countered that the Constitution was intended for humans only. The first patron reluctantly agreed . . . only to have a sudden brainstorm and bring up the fact that the Civil Rights Act outlawed discrimination on the basis of race. Also, he cleverly pointed out, Whilte was human (on his mother's side), so why couldn't he run? To ban him from running would be discriminatory and unconstitutional, pure and simple.

A third patron pointed out that it wouldn't matter if Whilte stayed in or not. He assured everyone that only whacko "Goth freaks" and serial killers would vote a half-demon into the Highest Office. Even with a near-perfect political career and spotless record, he'd less popular than Bush II at the end of his second term. Whilte would never get anything done in office, because who'd want to be seen as supporting a Hell-spawned politician?

That pretty much shut everyone up.

Then the TV caught everyone's attention with a breaking announcement. Nathan Whilte had just been assassinated, while giving yet another speech defending his right to run for President. His killer—an ex-Marine with a sniper rifle, no less—quietly surrendered two minutes later. A third patron tactlessly muttered her joy that Whilte hadn't been murdered near a grassy knoll.

Ironically, the stern-faced reporter announced Whilte's poll numbers had just started to make a rebound that very day.

I GIVE UP

Marlon Brikes, a.k.a. "SledgeChain," slowly approached the Paradise Hills police station on a pleasant spring morning. Along the way, passersby got the hell out of his way—or simply ran off. There were many reasons. One, he and his tattered blue maintenance uniform were covered in freshly-dried blood. Two, SledgeChain was a huge bastard with a 6'5", 290-pound frame of pure muscle. Three, there was the blood-covered fencing mask attached to his face via six evenly-spaced metal bolts screwed into his skull. Four, SledgeChain reeked in such a way that when he passed an old blind lady, she caught a whiff and vomited. Lastly, there was the thick, five-foot length of chain that he leisurely slung over his right shoulder, which had been welded to a metal sledgehammer head.

Dried blood also decorated the homemade weapon.

A few cops were enjoying a smoke outside when he walked passed them. They dropped their cigarettes and then drew their guns as SledgeChain headed inside. His description was well-known. The FBI had a special task force solely devoted to ending his six-state murder spree.

While this particular psycho used everything from axes to paper clips to kill his seventy-nine known victims, he was called SledgeChain for a reason. During each of his six killing sprees, one of his unlucky victims was singled out, nailed to a wall, and then beaten to death with his unique weapon.

But today, the mass murderer surrendered his weapon at the metal detector, shrugged when his fencing mask set it off anyway, and then made his way to the front desk. By this time, two dozen cops had pistols aimed his way. The call had gone out to SWAT as

SledgeChain approached the desk sergeant and turned himself in. They read him his rights, hosed him down (twice), gave him a change of clothes, and then booked him.

Detectives Duane Gaulm and Lucia Dimonyes waited in Interrogation Room B, tasked with the "honor" of questioning the prisoner. Dimonyes was an attractive, ponytailed Latina in gray slacks, a white blouse, and a black pair of reading glasses. Just shy of thirty-four, she sat at a long, rectangular table and skimmed through SledgeChain's thick file with quiet fascination. Gaulm was a tall, thin black man with short graying hair, a broken-in blue suit, and worry lines from his fifteen years on the force. In his late forties, he nervously paced about the room.

While they were both armed, Gaulm knew it wouldn't matter. He eyed the one-way mirror and reminded himself that six guys from SWAT were on the other side of it with authorization to fire on SledgeChain should he step out of line. Then he also remembered that guns didn't help the police in Hot Springs, South Dakota.

Nine months ago, SledgeChain walked in through the front door of their tiny sheriff's station and killed eight officers—along with four prisoners they had in lockup (one of whom was "sledgechained"). By the time backup could arrive, the killer was long-gone. Security footage chronicled most of the slaughter, including the part where the now-dead officers uselessly pumped over one hundred rounds into SledgeChain— only to end up crushed like insects.

The interrogation room's door opened.

A pair of burly officers escorted SledgeChain into the room. The orange jumpsuit they put him in strained to cover his bulk. While he wore manacles over his wrists and ankles, he even intimidated Dimonyes. The murderer looked like a poster child for steroid use. The skin on his hands was parchment-colored and just about as dry in appearance. Odd, patterned scars surrounded his exposed neck, reminding Gaulm of barbed wire scars. One of the killer's brown eyes was visible through a small hole in his battered fencing mask (still attached). The two cops kept their tasers out and ready until SledgeChain sat down. With a nod from Gaulm, they gratefully left the room.

"I'm Detective Gaulm," he briskly announced. "This is my partner, Detective Dimonyes."

SledgeChain's gaze roved between the two detectives.

"Would you like something to eat or drink?" Dimonyes asked.

SledgeChain shook his head.

"I guess we can get started then," Dimonyes said, forcing a smile. Gaulm headed for the corner farthest from SledgeChain, folded his arms, and kept his right hand close to his shoulder-holstered Glock .40.

"Why did you turn yourself in?" Dimonyes asked.

"Because I'm finished," SledgeChain replied with a deep, rumbling voice.

"Finished with what?" she pressed.

SledgeChain looked down at the table.

"Revenge," the killer uttered with a hint of satisfaction. "I found the last of them three hours ago. The one who struck the match. I made him suffer worse than the others."

Gaulm approached the table, an anxious look on his face. No one had reported any murders in their vicinity—yet. If SledgeChain was on foot, his victims had to be nearby.

"You just pulled off another killing spree?" Gaulm asked, with a quick glance toward the one-way glass. Hopefully, someone was acting on this new information.

"Yes."

"Where?" Gaulm pressed.

"St. Vincent's Sanitarium," the mass murderer evenly replied. "3146 Hollisway Path."

"Get some cars out there," Gaulm told Dimonyes. Reluctantly, the junior detective nodded and headed for the door. Her background in aberrant psychology made the prospect of interviewing SledgeChain downright compelling . . . but duty called. There might be survivors this time, although none were ever found at any of the other crime scenes. As Dimonyes exited the room, Gaulm glared at SledgeChain, with the evident temptation of testing the killer's "invulnerability" to gunfire. Then he took a deep breath and moved across the table from SledgeChain.

"How many dead?" Gaulm asked.

"Twenty-seven. I spared most of the patients," SledgeChain replied.

"Why?"

"Lunatics are people, too," the killer replied. "I was in such a good mood that I almost spared the staff. Almost."

"Why didn't you?"

"I killed them because I needed them dead," SledgeChain replied. "Besides, they might have ruined my plans, once they heard Ollins screaming."

"Who's Ollins?"

"Edward Ollins was the last of them. Once they doused and hung me with barbed wire, he struck the match."

The detective chewed the cryptic words in his head for a moment—especially that double reference to the struck match.

"So all of this is because someone tried to kill you?" Gaulms reasoned.

SledgeChain shook his head.

"No, detective. They actually killed me."

Gaulms frowned.

"You don't believe me?" SledgeChain asked, as if he had a smile under his mask. "Check my pulse."

The killer held out his manacled wrists. At first, Gaulm didn't move, even though his cop's curiosity tugged at him.

"Come on, detective," the killer teased. "I don't bite."

Slowly, Gaulm walked around the table and drew his gun. He carefully approached the motionless killer, then felt for a pulse along SledgeChain's left wrist.

Nothing.

In fact, SledgeChain's skin was frigid. Gaulm actually wriggled his fingers to regain feeling in them. Stranger still was the fact that the air around him was at normal room temperature.

"I've been dead for eleven-and-a-half years, "SledgeChain declared, "since one night in October."

"Who killed you?"

"A bunch of punks, detective," SledgeChain replied. "I was homeless at the time, trying to find work. They found me sleeping in an alley and decided to have some fun. So they beat me, hung me, and left me to burn."

"What happened next?" Gaulm asked.

"I went to Hell."

"I'm not surprised," Gaulm said with disgust, as he stepped away from the killer and holstered his gun.

"I was," SledgeChain sighed. "I used to be a good man. Went to church every Sunday. Never hurt anyone. Yet, I went to Hell."

"Why?"

"It was explained to me that the cruelty of my death was so great that it stained my soul. My anger, my rage, was so great that it had damned me. Souls like mine were given a rare choice: eternal torment or a chance at revenge."

"So you died really pissed off?" Gaulm scoffed. "That was good enough to get you an express pass out of Hell?"

"I didn't make the rules," SledgeChain replied with a shrug. "When I came back, I found out that my conscience was completely gone. I also realized that I needed to feed in order to stay remain here."

"How do you feed exactly?"

"I've fed on everyone I've ever killed," replied the killer. "Their souls sustained me while I tracked down my murderers. After the first two killing sprees, the others knew for certain that I was after them and did their best to hide."

"You sound like you're full of shit," Gaulm sneered. "I just thought you might want to know that."

"Madelyn Willis," SledgeChain coolly announced. "She was one of the sanitarium staffers I killed last night. The slippery minx almost managed to get away. At the moment, she's digesting. Want to meet her?"

Gaulm nodded as his fingers hovered near his gun again.

SledgeChain looked down at his palms, which he held parallel to each other—roughly six inches apart. There was a flash of reddish-orange light and a tiny, ghostly image of a woman appeared. Dressed in a white nurse's attire, Madelyn was covered with blood. In her

apparent fifties, the staffer floated between
SledgeChain's palms—minus her left arm.
"This is Madelyn's soul . . . what's left of it."
Morbidly fascinated, Gaulm came in a bit closer.
She looked like a holographic projection of some
kind, which wasn't possible. SledgeChain had been
searched from top-to-bottom. Then she actually saw
Gaulm and screamed something toward him. Yet her
pleading voice didn't carry into the room. Gaulm
shuddered at the sight.
"What happened to her arm?" The detective quietly
asked.
"I beat her to death with it," SledgeChain bragged.
"It's not as easy as you'd think."
"Now what?" Gaulm replied. "You're going back
to Hell?"
"I would deserve it, wouldn't I?"
SledgeChain slapped his palms together and
Madelyn's disembodied scream filled the room. The
masked killer inhaled deeply and reclined in his chair.
"Female souls are so . . . delicious. Did you know
that—?"
"Not meaning to interrupt," Gaulm pressed. "But
aren't you supposed to be going back to Hell now?"
"That would be the right thing to do," the killer
admitted, "but I had a better idea."
"And what's that?" Gaulm asked.
"I need to clean up my karma a bit. So I made a
call before I turned myself in."
"What kind of call?"
"Think of it as a phone interview, Detective Gaulm.
I simply offered my services, in exchange for a few
intangible benefits."
"To whom?!" Gaulm incredulously asked. "No
one's crazy enough to hire a monster like you!"

"You'd be surprised, Detective Gaulm," SledgeChain replied. Almost on cue, the door opened and in walked three men in suits. Their look screamed "feds" to the seasoned detective. One of them flashed a CIA badge and transfer orders. As Gaulm examined the orders, he put himself in SledgeChain's shoes. If he continued to aimlessly wander about killing people, sooner or later someone might get lucky and cap his ass. Then he'd surely go to back to Hell—probably for good.

So why not kill for the "good guys"?

The captain came in and verified the transfer orders. Gaulm stepped aside and let the feds take custody of their "prisoner." Gaulm turned to face the undead killer, who rose to his ominous height. The detective could've sworn that SledgeChain's visible eye winked at him on the way out.

MESSY

"Some people just don't like change," I mused aloud.

Tony Webber whimpered nearby. The 50 year-old cybergenetics designer looked scholarly enough in his gray pajamas, thick-rimmed glasses, and curly blonde hair. The poor fella had a painful decision to make. He'd either give up his life's dream or watch his family die. The way things were going, he was leaning for the latter.

We commandeered a car wash for tonight's negotiations. His wife (Juliette) and two college-aged sons (Isaac and Quincy) were chained to some kind of conveyor rig. Drenched in water and soap, they whimpered through their gags and blindfolds. I sat with Webber and three of my new triggers in the waiting area. Comfy and dry, we watched his family through a room-length wall of glass.

"Your symbiote's almost a century ahead of its time," I continued. "Assuming it didn't put existing augmentation firms out of business, there's the big picture. Anyone with that thing would be damned-near un-killable."

Webber gave me a strange look as I mentioned that last part, like a mad scientist who wanted to rant about his toy—but was just smart enough not to.

"The first nation to mass-produce your symbiote could seriously fuck up the world, Mr. Webber. While I'm no hero, I like the world very much the way it is."

"Goddamn Colombians," Webber cursed. "They sent you, didn't they?"

Being the discreet fixer I was, I didn't bother to reply (but yeah—they sent me).

"Tell you what," offered Webber, "keep me alive and you and I can be partners! We could make billions overnight!"

My guys chuckled in the background. They had been with me long enough to know that I didn't take bribes from a mark. Ever. Besides, I was already a billionaire. Being a fixer meant servicing other people's sins. I could have a kidnapped child rescued, start an ethnic cleansing, and everything in-between. I was the best in the game, which meant I had the best talent and could charge obscene fees to work miracles. Good or evil didn't matter to me—only the details of the job and the asking price.

I lit a Marlboro as Webber ranted on about the bullshit notion of being a 50/50 partner. Even if I was greedy enough to screw the Colombians, Webber had already killed his last two partners after tricking them out of their just shares.

"So do we have a deal, Mr. Cly?" Webber asked with a hopeful smile.

"Money's changed hands, Mr. Webber," I muttered. "So much money that I'm personally handling this job."

Webber's face reddened with frustrated ire. I could sympathize. Normally, I'd just have my telepaths pluck the knowledge from his mind. Yet the clever fuck had himself psi-screened with fail safes. Basically, his brain would permanently turn off if anyone breached his mental defenses or subjected him torture. It was a fact he mentioned often, even on Twitter.

Thus far, my forensic folks could only find scraps of symbiote research, which my super geniuses declared to be both amazingly advanced and almost impossible to reverse-engineer. The only thing they knew for certain was that Webber wasn't smart enough to have designed it himself. Odds were that someone had been born with the damned thing. Webber could've just cut it out of some poor super and worked on reproducing it.

For that much money, I would've.

"If I give in, you'll kill me," Webber said.

It was funny how he didn't mention the wife or sons.

"You don't understand, Mr. Webber," I replied, exhaling smoke. "Under the terms of this job, the symbiote is kind of a bonus."

Webber's face fell as he realized that I was dead-serious.

"Give it up and we're gone," I smirked, figuring that it would take years for him to replace the tech—if ever.

Poor Webber looked me in the eye . . . and attacked.

One moment, he was sitting next to me, a mousy little man. The next, the fucker was seven feet tall and ripped from head-to-toe. His pajamas exploded Hulk-style as Webber snatched me up by the throat. Before my cigarette hit the floor, my shooters expertly tagged him with non-lethal shots. The bullets harmlessly flattened against Webber's altered physique.

With a triumphant grin, the geneticist used me as a human shield.

"Drop your guns or he dies!" Webber threatened, eyes glowing with red menace . . . oh right. The heat beams.

Most mercs would've been confused and scared. Instead, two of them aimed at his family. The third one just shook his head and laughed. With a frown, Webber looked down at me. Then he got the joke. Too busy making threats, the geneticist hadn't seen my suit in action.

A two-piece Armani knockoff, I never left home without it. The sucker armored up whenever I was in imminent danger (like now). Every inch of skin was now covered in silvery nanites. Having been run over by a train once, I wasn't too afraid of Mr. Webber. Still, I could do without any more violence. Since I knew what his powers were, I didn't bother gazing them over . . . I merely ripped them away and quickly rendered them passive. Webber was suddenly his old self again. "Impossible!" Webber yelped. "What did you do to my symbiote?!"

"Nothing," I lied as the nanites receded from my face. "Must've been a dud prototype."

Funny how broken he suddenly looked. Ah well. Half of what kept me alive was not flaunting my abilities. This new face and burger gut allowed me to stay under the radar and ply my black ops training to make a villainous buck. Once the nanites receded into my suit, I grabbed Webber's left wrist and twisted it in an unnatural angle. Bones snapped as he screamed and dropped to both knees.

"Kill me and you'll never get my research!" Webber bluffed through sobbing and bitch tears.

My power rip should last five hours. Yet, since my powers were starting to fail, I'd have Webber dosed with inhibitor serum just to be safe. I gave my shooters the nod and snapped my fingers. Two of them nodded as they grabbed the dumb fuck and dragged him away.

A snap of the fingers was my equivalent to "kiss of death" for a target. The third shooter waited until Webber was out of the room.

"What about them?" he asked, expecting a kill order.

I gave the hostages a glance. Dead witnesses were easier to manage but I didn't work that way. Being a high-end fixer meant working by different rules.

"Wipe their memories and cut 'em loose," I muttered as I fished out another cigarette. "They're better off without that limp prick."

THE WINNING TICKET

The neighborhood tavern was all-but empty, as it was the lapse between Happy Hour and Monday Night Football. Inside, Glen tended bar with hasty precision. In his mid-twenties, Glen was a womanizing college grad out of Michigan State University with an International Business degree . . . who realized that bartending was more fun.

Ivan Hursner entered with a look of pure self-loathing and sat at the bar without pause or greeting. Short, fat, and balding, he looked to be in his early 40's. Having just braved the rush-hour tedium, Hursner still wore his gray maintenance uniform. Glen poured him a glass of *Miller Light*, his usual brand. The bartender knew all too well of Ivan's never-ending misfortunes.

His luck went south over a year ago.

Ivan got laid off from his good-paying job at the *Ford* plant. His two-timing wife left him, took the kids, and somehow gotten the house in the divorce settlement. As Glen recalled, Ivan's ex then sold the house (that he paid for) for a loss, moved the kids to Phoenix, and was dating half the male population out there.

Ivan had to move back in with his parents.

His debts spiraled in the year it took him to find his current job as a custodian at a public high school— which paid far less than he used to make. In Detroit, life could be quite dangerous. Ivan was almost shot twice, (actually) stabbed twice, robbed five times, and used as a human shield four times . . . and that was just when he was at work.

His nagging father had a stroke and died in his sleep a year later. Soon after the funeral, his half-senile mother completely flipped out and had to be committed. Thus, Ivan inherited his parents' debts, owed child support on two kids he couldn't afford to see, and suffered a truly hostile work environment. Times like these made Glen thrilled to be a bartender. Other people's pathetic tales of woe made him feel so much better about his own existence.

"On me man," Glen offered as Ivan sat at the bar.

"Thanks," Ivan mumbled as he gratefully accepted the glass and took a sip.

Glen studied Ivan's pitiful expression and realized that this was over-and-beyond the standard bad day.

"What happened now?"

"Remember that record-setting $500 million-dollar lottery jackpot from last year?"

Did he? Glen sank $100 bucks worth of bar tips into tickets. He heard that one lucky bastard hit— somewhere in Detroit, no less. Last he heard, no one had stepped up and claimed the jackpot.

"Yeah. So?"

Ivan reached into his pocket and pulled out an old lottery ticket. Glen's jaw dropped as he connected the dots.

"No way!"

Ivan slapped it on the bar for Glen to see. Glen picked up and eyed the coffee-stained ticket.

"It's 16 months old. Useless. Not worth the paper it's printed on." Ivan said before he took a long sip. "God hates me."

Glen shook his head with amazement as he handed the ticket back.

"How'd you not know that you won the lottery?!"

"Well, the guys at work had this lottery pool. I pitched my money in every week. Once in a blue moon, we'd split a hundred-dollar prize or something but we never won anything big. When this jackpot came up, I put one dollar on one ticket: just for me. When I lost it, I figured it was a losing ticket and forgot about it."

"Where'd you find it?" Glen asked.

"I'll get to that," Ivan replied as he pocketed the ticket. "Anyway, I was driving my mom's car the day I bought the ticket. Her car's transmission broke down the day before I could get my car out of the shop. So I got it towed into the backyard. In the midst of all this, the damned ticket slipped under the front seat!"

"Damn!" Glen gawked with amazement, knowing that he'd be repeating this story for at least a year . . .

"About sixteen months later, I finally got around to scrapping the car. As I was cleaning it out, I found the ticket, got curious, and checked the number online. When I realized that I had the winning ticket, I called the Lottery Commission. They laughed their asses off at me."

Ivan dejectedly sipped his beer.

"I must've been a Nazi in a past life or something."

The business grad sighed as he paused and regarded the ceiling for a moment.

"You're looking at this all wrong," Glen advised with a sudden, inspired smile.

"How's that?"

"You've got yourself one fucked-up story here," Glen argued. "Spin it right and you could make some money off it. A book deal or one of those reality shows. Think about it: not everybody loses a half-billion-dollar payday."

"No," Ivan emphatically shook his head. "My life's humiliating enough. I don't need to make a reality show about it."

"But you need to make some money, right?"

"Why take the chance?" Ivan replied. "Everything I touch turns to ash, Glen."

The poor guy downed his beer and stood up.

"Want another one?" Glen asked. "You've got the God-given right to get shitfaced tonight."

"No thanks," sighed Ivan. "Evening mass starts in an hour. Then I've got to help serve food at Haven of Charity."

Ivan left the bar and headed for his car. Along the way, he stepped on a large pile of fresh dog shit. With a groan of disgust, he scraped as much of it as he could off his left boot. Then he found a parking ticket on the windshield of his battered white Toyota. Ivan glanced around and realized that he had parked next to a fire hydrant that hadn't been there yesterday. He merely sighed, took the parking ticket, and slid it into his uniform's left breast pocket.

"Gimme your keys!" A male voice yelled from behind as the barrel of a gun was jammed against the back of Ivan's spine.

Ivan suppressed a chuckle as he pulled out his keys, took off his cheap watch, and handed his nearly-empty wallet over his right shoulder. They were rudely snatched away. Ivan raised his hands, closed his eyes, and calmly stepped over to his right. He heard the mugger hop into his car and speed off.

At least I won't have to worry about the brakes, Ivan mused to himself.

Six seconds later, the sky suddenly opened up. Cold, stinging rain pour down upon Ivan with a chilling wrath. He opened his eyes, stoically pulled a pack of cinnamon gum out of his back pocket, and had a piece.

"Kill yourself already!" Ethudahl screamed into Ivan's right ear.

A very frustrated, managerial-ranked Angel of Death, Ethudahl wore a nice gray suit and tie. His wings were black, his wavy red hair was combed back, and his halo golden. He appeared to be in his mid-fifties . . . but he was actually much older.

Next to him stood Mariel. The ancient, gorgeous Angel of Death looked to be in her mid-thirties with wings and a halo like Ethudahl's. The blonde aide wore an all-crimson corporate pantsuit with matching heels and a pair of black, horn-rimmed glasses.

The downpour fell through both angels, who stood perfectly dry. A miserably-wet couple held hands as they ran through Mariel and toward the bar to get out of the rain. Ivan continued to stand where he was, as if enjoying a shower.

"What else should I try, sir?" Mariel asked.

"I don't know!" Ethudahl fumed. "The lottery ticket would've made most people eat a bullet!"

"Hursner's a really good Catholic, sir," Mariel reasoned. "Suicide's against his grain."

Ethudahl turned on Mariel with such a glare that she flinched.

"I don't care if he's the Pope! We've got a quota to fill!" Ethudahl screamed as he angrily pointed at Ivan. "And this dumb brick of a man was supposed to kill himself over a year ago!"

If God hadn't personally cast Ethudahl out of Heaven among the ranks of the Fallen, he'd pray to the bastard for guidance right now. Ivan Hursner was destined for Hell via suicide. The mortal's case file had already gone through the hands of three subordinate Angels of Death. When it came to getting people to commit suicide, Ethudahl was the best . . . which was why Ivan's case ended up on his desk.

"I could have his parents' house burned down or get him laid off again," Mariel offered.

Ethudahl pulled a pack of cigarettes out of thin air and fired one up with a fancy gold lighter (also conjured from nothingness).

"He'd expect those things to happen," Ethudahl scowled. "It's probably why he spends so much time at the homeless shelter, the slippery prick!"

Ivan still stood there in the rain, oblivious to the pair of angels nearby. Ethudahl blew ethereal smoke into Ivan's face.

"A bout of cancer, maybe?" Ethudahl asked.

"I looked into it, sir, but our budget won't sustain it. And Fatal Diseases hates sharing kills with us at the tail-end of a quarterly cycle."

"They would. What about maiming him with a hit-n-run?"

"Maiming isn't returning my calls. They're very short-staffed."

"Did you try Accidents?" Ethudahl asked.

"Yes. They're even more backlogged than Maiming. I heard they're hiring temps."

"For Hell's sake!" Ethudahl exclaimed as he glared at Ivan. "Suicide's supposed to be the best department in the game! We're efficient! Tidy! We rack up a Hell-bound body count second to none . . . except for Murder, Accidents, Starvation and Fatal Diseases! But this one, lard-assed bastard won't off himself like he's supposed to! He's making us a laughingstock, Mariel!"

"There was one sub-department capable of fast-tracking him," she hesitantly offered.

Ethudahl turned toward her with wild hope in his eyes.

"Who?! Animal Maulings? Riots? Product Recalls?"

"No on all counts," she swallowed nervously. "Decadent Lifestyles has a few slots to fill, with the recent batch of celebrity deaths."

Ethudahl paused and seriously considered the option.

Mariel was surprised.

Normally, he'd fly into a rage whenever she even mentioned them. Decadent Lifestyles was considered a joke of a sub-department because they didn't actually kill people. They oversaw deaths by the hell-bound rich and famous. When their time came, Decadent Lifestyles would close the deal by setting up their "clients" to die in a tragic/silly/memorable fashion and allow another department to close the deal.

Sometimes, they spent years setting up someone's decline. Other times, their target's downfall was far too abrupt. Still, their results were quite newsworthy in the mortal tabloids. The other departments preferred to keep Decadent Lifestyles at arm's length because it was considered a sign of incompetence to fully partner up with them. And their staffers were somewhat . . . eccentric (even among the Fallen).

But Ethudahl was desperate.

"What did you have in mind?" Ethudahl asked.

"What if poor Ivan suddenly fell into money and fame—perhaps, with unscrupulous people all around him? Maybe someone gets him hooked on drugs, he gets his heart broken, falls into a bout of depression, and then ultimately offs himself?"

Ethudahl found the idea repulsive. His tried-and-true method was to make a target's life so miserable that he/she would opt for suicide over living another hour. People from all walks of life ended up damning themselves for eternity—all because of his "tinkering." He prided himself as an artist, whose talents had raised him to his current position faster than any of his predecessors. Ethudahl was a professional with a glowing track record and senior management potential. He heard whispers of promotion in the wind . . .

Then along came Ivan Hursner.

The longest he had ever taken to "off" someone was eleven days—and that was during the Black Plague. The

Ivan had to come along and stain his flawless record. Instead of promotion rumors, Ethudahl now heard of a new interdepartmental pool. And they weren't betting on how long it would take for Ivan to die. Rather, they were betting on how long it would take for Ethudahl to lose his job. He was being watched by his superiors, who were far from happy with him right now.

Ivan Hursner had single-handedly driven Suicide's budget through the roof. If Ethudahl couldn't take him out within the next three quarterly cycles, he was done for. The Fallen would have to think way outside of the box this time. Then his desperate mind remembered a detail about Ivan Hursner.

The mortal was actually destined to win that massive jackpot and find the ticket before it expired. Rewriting Ivan's destiny put a wicked dent into their budget. Now, it just might be what Ethudahl needed to put Ivan down for good. He'd then spin the results to make it look like a massive triumph over a worthy mortal adversary.

Then, once Hursner killed himself and his soul was safely bound to Hell, Ethudahl would personally whip him with molten chains in his spare time. That satisfaction was a small price to pay for dealing with Decadent Lifestyles.

"Do it," Ethudahl said firmly.

"Consider it done," Mariel replied. She pulled out a cell phone and hit the speed-dial.

Roughly a minute later, Glen rushed out under a black umbrella, with an awed smile on his face. He found Ivan, who still basked in the rain, and ran over to him.

"Ivan!"

Ivan opened his eyes and turned around.
"I checked the jackpot win date online. Your
ticket's still good!"
"What?!" Ivan asked, his face twisted with shock.
"Your ticket: it's only 11 months old!"
Ivan pulled the lottery ticket out of his pocket and
eyed the date under the pouring rain. He would've
sworn that the date was different . . .
"I won the lottery?" Ivan asked, a cautious smile
creeping across his face.
"Yes you did, Ivan!" Glen exclaimed, as he put an
umbrella over both Glen and his precious prize ticket.
"You're a rich man!"
Ivan and Glen shared a laugh in the rain.
"See?" Glen slapped Ivan on the back. "God
doesn't hate you after all!"
"You might be right," Ivan replied with a flicker of
long-forgotten hope in his heart, as he and Glen went
back inside the bar.
Behind them, Ethudahl gave Ivan an evil smile and
thought of molten chains.
Mariel put her cell phone away with a mischievous
grin, hoping that Ivan could hold out just a bit longer.
She'd already gone behind Ethudahl's back and cut a
side deal with Decadent Lifestyles. Ivan would get rich,
slip into a decadence that would make Elvis cringe, and
then get his heart broken by some whore.
But instead of killing himself out of despair, Mariel
would twist events. Instead of a suicide, Ivan would die
pushing someone out of the path of an oncoming truck.
While he'd still die, that kind of self-sacrifice that would
send him straight to Heaven.
After a screw-up like that, Ethudahl's career would
be done for certain . . . allowing Mariel to take his
infernal desk.

THE COLONY

The British colony ship *Thames* exited through the wormhole at maximum thrust. Large and sleek, the blue-hulled vessel was surrounded by a form-fitting defensive shield of transparent energy. As the wormhole closed behind them, the shield flickered visibly and then collapsed. The ship's twelve rear thrusters also extinguished one-by-one, along with most of the vessel's multiple external lights.

Inside the vessel, Captain Mortimer Sykes slowly rose to his feet, followed by most of the bridge staff. A stout Brit in his late 50's, Sykes wore the standard green-and-blue uniform of the British Interstellar Navy. He touched his bald head and felt a trickle of blood just above his left eyebrow. Other than that, some aches along his backside, and a serious desire for a pint, he felt perfectly fine.

A quick glance around the large, ovular bridge told him that no one was dead. Although his second-in-command—Commander McGooter—howled in shrill agony as she clutched her right leg. Sparks flickered from numerous duty stations. The damage was probably ship-wide, considering the amount of pounding their shields took. Medics rushed onto the bridge. One of them headed over to Sykes but was waved away.

"Damage report, Mr. Clarke," Sykes winced.

The blonde-haired status officer was already at a sensor console with a look of disbelief on his face. He was so absorbed that he didn't hear the order.

"Mr. Clarke?" Captain Sykes repeated with emphasis. "Status?"

"Sorry sir," Clarke turned away from the console. "Damage assessments are coming in now. Engines are down. Shields are down. Weapons—much to my

amazement—are operational. Minor hull breaches in
Sections 12 and 51. Standard power's at 34%. Full
emergency power's been diverted to the cryo-bunkers.
No fatalities there, sir. Crew counts—so far—show
nonlethal injuries."
Sykes owed the chaps in Engineering a bottle of
finely-aged scotch when this was over. He had a crew of
894 and another 34,612 colonists in stasis. After the
beating the *Thames* had taken, he was surprised that they
all hadn't ended up a cloud of expanding gases by now.
While en route to the Avalon Colony, they ran into an
unstable wormhole while in hyperspace—something the
spatial theorists claimed was impossible. With a
lifespan of about fourteen hours, the phenomenon didn't
show up on their sensors. Unable to back out of it, they
"rode the rapids" and punched through the bloody thing.
"Where are we now?"
Clarke hit a few keys, hesitated, and rechecked his
readings.
"You won't believe this," the junior officer
muttered as he hit a few more buttons and raised the
bridge's blast shields. As the metal barriers rose,
everyone could see through the transparent nanoglass
and viewed a blue-green planet. Based on the formation
of the continents, the planet was clearly Earth. The
mystified bridge crew eyed the blue-green orb in silence.
Even McGooter, who was being carried away on a
stretcher, stopped her shrieking and gawked at the sight.
"Is that Earth?" Sykes softly asked.
"Yes sir," Clarke nodded, as he entered new
commands into his console. "Based on current stellar
movements, I'd estimate that we're in the 10th century,
A.D."
"Recheck your readings," Sykes murmured, fairly
certain that Clarke wasn't wrong. The proof was right in

front of him. They were in the past because Earth wasn't a giant debris field—like it "was" in his time.
"Readings are triple-confirmed, sir," Clarke replied.
"Magnify image," Sykes ordered.
Another officer hit a few buttons and the distant planet abruptly looked very close. So close that they could see England. It was beautiful—far more so than in the historical vids he'd seen as a child. Fatigued and distracted, the Captain gave a string of orders, primarily geared toward ship repairs.
"I think I need a drink and a long nap," Sykes wearily declared as he winced and headed for the exit. "Mr. Clarke, you have the bridge. Continue repairs, keep word of this contained, and for the love of God no 'field trips' while I'm asleep!"
"Aye, sir," Clarke replied with a smile.

Six hours later, Sykes returned to the bridge with an adhesive bandage over his cut. A few pills and some much-needed sleep had him feeling mostly normal. He was impressed to see that the bridge looked almost completely repaired.
"Captain on deck!" an anonymous crewman shouted.
Everyone snapped to attention.
"At ease," Sykes ordered as he walked over to his chair and sat down. "What's our status, Mr. Clarke?"
"Shields are fully-operational. Standard power's at full again. Hyperdrive will be restored within the hour," Clarke reported. "Engineering estimates another eleven hours before the hull breach can be fully-repaired. No fatalities. But we have twenty-six injured in the infirmary stations."
"Anything serious?"

"Three engineers suffered radiation burns. I was told they'll pull through but will need some extensive surgery, sir."
"I see," Sykes sighed. "Keep me posted on their condition. Now, have you confirmed that we are indeed in the 10th century?"
"Roughly mid-August of 969 A.D., sir."
"Damn," Sykes chuckled. "We're far too early for the Battle of Hastings."
"It's quite tempting, isn't it sir?" Clarke mused.
"How's that, Commander?"
"Well, here we are with a soon-to-be-fully-functional vessel. Down there's our home, which will someday be reduced to tiny bits. Makes me wonder if we couldn't make things better, sir?"
"Like how?" Sykes chuckled. "Starting the British Empire a bit early? Settling North America before Columbus is born? Stopping the Black Plague or the Inquisitions?"
"For starters sir," Clarke replied. "Maybe we can even save our home world in the process."
Sykes could see that Clarke was dead-serious. A quick glance around the bridge told him that other members of his crew felt the same way. They must have had some lively conversations in his absence. The captain realized that it had been a mistake to take a nap without settling this matter beforehand.
He'd have to do so now.
"Unfortunately, Mr. Clarke, it wouldn't do to mess around with history. Such an action—however well-intentioned—might actually make things worse. For one thing, we might erase ourselves from the time stream. Another's that our ancestors might end up getting their hands on some of our technology and blow up the Earth a thousand years ahead of schedule."

Sykes stood up and gestured toward the image of the Earth. "Everything we are came from their triumphs and failures. And we're better for it, Mr. Clarke. Let's not risk tampering with that."

Clarke reluctantly nodded.

"Orders then, sir?"

"We set course for Avalon," Sykes ordered. "We'll stretch our legs there for a few months, mine some rethox ore for the reactors, and then move on."

"On to where, sir?"

"Past the Galactic Brink," Sykes replied as he folded his arms. "There are probably a few habitable worlds we haven't bothered to discover yet, Mr. Clarke. Who knows? Perhaps one of them will make a rather nice home."

"Aye, sir."

Sykes sat down as an ensign handed him a list of orders to sign. Clarke turned back to his duty station to hide his frustration. While the captain had a point, the old man was being naïve. When the superpowers nuked the Earth in 2419, ten billion people died. Had his parents not been honeymooning on Zentares Colony, Clarke would never have been born. The way he saw it, Fate had brought them here for a reason. During the captain's nap, Clarke had brought the issue up with the *Thames'* other key officers—all of whom saw things his way. Most were eager to set foot on Earth and breathe in the air of their home world for the first time.

Odds were that the colonists would want to do the same thing, if given a choice. But he could already see that Captain Sykes wouldn't let them remain on Avalon either, simply to preserve that world's historical purity as well. This being the first known case of time travel, there weren't any regulations regarding interactions with the time stream. Sykes was simply running on the premise that time wasn't meant to be tampered with.

But what the captain didn't take into account was the fact that none of them really wanted to traipse off into the unknown. What if they ran into some other spatial phenomenon and the *Thames* took even more damage—perhaps too much to repair? They could die in the middle of space, far from anywhere. Therefore, by the time the *Thames* made it to Avalon, Clarke's mutiny would be planned and ready to go. Some of the crew would follow the old man but they could be taken without too many casualties. When it was over, the prisoners would be placed in stasis. The rest of the crew could then build up a colony on Avalon, manufacture more starships, and return to Earth. Instead of directly colonizing Earth, they'd sculpt its history from afar.

Their agents would be sent throughout the world, minimizing the lingering cultural divides which eventually doomed Earth. Also, the major superpowers would end up broken into smaller countries, without the capacity to ruin the world again. Even if things went horribly wrong and the crew erased themselves from the time stream, Clarke thought the effort to be worth the risk because he couldn't, in good conscience, abandon his home world to eventual oblivion.

Besides, how else was he ever going to make Captain?

THE CHECK'S IN THE MAIL

Reginald McDrell right-handedly dragged his latest victim across the cemetery's rain-soaked grass under a cool night sky. In his early forties, he had a large build and a ruggedly-cruel face. Reginald walked on a comfy pair of black steel-toed boots. His clothes were plain, sturdy, and dark-hued with a waist-length black jacket to keep out the October chill. Clipped to his belt was a red burner cell with a white earpiece wire running up to his right ear. A pair of 9mm pistols dangled from a double-shoulder rig under his jacket.

In his left hand was a jerry can of gasoline.

Dressed in mud-covered pink pajamas, this victim was a fourteen-year-old girl. After Reginald killed her parents, he spent a few minutes chasing her down. Then he beat her unconscious, breaking several bones in her little body. Long brown hair stuck to her broken, bloodied face. He had taken the effort to tie separate lengths of rope around her arms and ankles. Even though it had been a redundant gesture, Reginald even tied a blue cloth gag around her bruised mouth.

As he dragged her toward an empty grave, the cell phone rang. With a surprise frown, he stopped next to the hole and kicked her into it with just enough time to answer on the fourth ring.

"Hello?"

"Well hello yourself, you cheap bastard!"

Reginald inwardly groaned at the shrill sound of Dolores McDrell's voice. It hadn't struck him as shrill when they first met at a church picnic twelve years ago, or throughout their six-year marriage. Even when she divorced Reginald five years ago, took him for what little he had, and then nailed him for child support, her voice didn't bother him.

But by God, her voice had gotten damned shrill now! Since he went underground, Reginald had cut off all contact with his past. It was safer for all concerned. His new line of work was just too dangerous. Still, somehow, that honey-blonde bitch had reached out of his past and clawed at him with that damned shrill voice.

"Hey baby," Reginald replied as he unscrewed the can of gasoline. "How're the kids?"

"Much better off, now that you're gone!"

Reginald grinned. Dolores was probably right. He emptied the gas can into the little girl's grave (dug just for tonight). She awakened to the sting of premium unleaded being poured into her open facial cuts. The girl took a whiff of the gasoline and released a muffled scream as she tried to get free.

"Cool," Reginald replied. "How 'bout you, baby? How've you been?"

"Cut the bullshit! I want my money!"

He dropped the empty can onto the grave, pulled out a new pack of Marlboro menthols, and ripped it open.

"You sound like one of my old bookies," Reginald grinned as he slipped a cigarette into his mouth and dropped the rest of the cancer sticks into the grave. "How'd you get my number?"

"My brother's a P.I., remember?" Dolores gloated. "He tracked your sorry ass all the way down to Raleigh."

"Really?" Reginald replied, half-impressed.

He had always thought of her brother Brenton as a dumbass, who couldn't find the sun on a clear morning. Either Reginald had gotten sloppy or Brenton had gotten lucky—or maybe a bit of both. He'd have to look into that when he was done here.

"You must be rolling in the dough to be driving that fancy Mustang of yours," Dolores ranted.

Reginald pulled out his silver-plated Zippo lighter, with an emblem of a crucified Jesus on both sides. He flicked it open and produced a flame. Reginald thought of the 2016 Mustang, which he had stolen from another victim. He'd now have to ditch the vehicle and borrow Brenton's . . . once he tracked the idiot down.

"It's sort of a loaner," Reginald replied as he fired up his cigarette and took a deep drag. "And I'm gainfully unemployed, sweetheart."

"Don't give me that! You're working construction under the table, aren't you?! It's the only way you could afford a Mustang!"

Nice guess, Reginald thought to himself as he put his lighter away. Actually, he made a decent living from his victims, as part of his "roaming serial killer" cover. A fat wad of money rested in his underwear, keeping his hairy balls warm and uncomfortable.

Reginald hit the tiny light on his watch and took in the time. It was 12:06 a.m. back home. He could almost see her pacing outside of the trailer in one of her many knee-high nighties, trying not to wake the kids. Damn, she always did look good in a nightie!

"Okay sweetness, how much do I owe you?" Reginald asked as he suppressed a cough.

He had given up smoking about six months back. But lately, the "itch" to smoke a butt had taken hold of him. This would be his one indulgence to that urge. With a last, lusty exhalation, Reginald dropped the lit cigarette into the open grave and stepped back as flames shot forth. As her gag burned away, the girl screamed freely amidst the sudden fury of the modest inferno.

Dolores said something. But Reginald couldn't hear her over the noise.

"Sorry," Reginald said. "How much do I owe you?"

"$11,192 dollars, you prick!" Dolores repeated.

"Okay," Reginald replied. "I'll send you a check for an even twenty grand: for your mental anguish. Will that shut you up?"

There was a pause on the other end.

"Where'd you get twenty grand?"

Reginald could hear the greed in her voice, wondering how long Dolores would wait before she'd go to the judge and try to yank up his monthly payments again.

"I got lucky in a poker game," he lied. "And I walked away with about twenty-five large. So, what do you say?"

"That check better be in my mailbox in three days," came her reply.

"It's in the mail baby," Reginald promised before he hung up on her.

Even after eight seconds of burning from head-to-toe, the little girl screamed. *Poor thing*, Reginald thought to himself, as he watched her burn. Then he made a mental note to have Rome overnight a beer-stained cashier's check to the County Child Support people. If he sent it directly to Dolores, she'd cash the damned thing and claim that he had sent her nothing.

Maybe in his next life he'd be smart enough not to marry a hooker. At least she decided to give up prostitution after the wedding. Odds were that she was staying relatively clean now. Even at thirty-six, Dolores could've made a good living on the streets or hooked herself a new husband to leech off of.

But to track him down, all the way from Vegas, things must be tight. She might even still be working at the post office and feeding Michelle and Eric with an honest paycheck. Reginald changed his mind. He'd have Rome send her twenty-five.

For a brief moment, he toyed with the idea of looking in on his family—

Then the first vampire suddenly swooped out of the sky, a black-clad male with a thin build. His pale face was twisted with suppressed agony as he rushed Reginald with clawed hands and unnatural speed. Reginald whipped out his guns and cut loose with a flurry of wooden hollow point rounds. Each bullet was designed to penetrate and then shatter inside of a target. They were guaranteed to end a vampire's "immortal" life if they landed in a vital organ. And Reginald liked hollow points because there'd be few—if any—exit wounds. The ex-smoker grinned as the dead bloodsucker staggered backwards and died without a fuss. White smoke sizzled from his slack mouth and six chest wounds.

Unable to die from normal flames, the charred little (vampire) girl continued to scream. Reginald turned toward the grave and stifled the temptation to be merciful and put a round into her head. He couldn't do that because she was the bait.

All vampires in a nest had a tight psychic link to each other, allowing them to find each other with ease. The link also established a sort of hierarchy among them. Whoever created the nest controlled every subordinate vampire within it. Someone new—like the little girl—was at the bottom of the hierarchy. Given time and a bunch of new converts, she would've been able to bend newer vamplings to her will.

What Reginald liked about the link was its unique flaw. Torture one of them and you torture all of them. Since one of these monsters had turned the girl and her parents, this link made hunting them a lot easier. Another dozen vampires landed around him and moved in swiftly for the kill: eight males and four females. Each of them looked to be in exquisite agony, no doubt because of the little vampire girl's suffering.

"Engage!" Reginald yelled as he threw himself backwards, his arms folded across his chest with pistols still in hand. His backup team popped up from their distant points of concealment and opened fire. Caught off-guard, the vampires hissed and died as modified assault rifle rounds—explosive-tipped and filled with garlic powder—connected with their pale bodies and exploded. The garlic was like a poisonous acid, destroying vital organs upon contact. Since his teammates were each skilled marksmen, Reginald felt safe under their well-aimed crossfire, as the last of the vamps went down around him.

The vampire hunter rose to his feet, brushed some grass clippings from his clothes, and gave the "all clear" signal. A six-man team stepped out of the darkness. Each man wore dark green face paint, Ghillie suits, and tactical gear. They reloaded and cautiously approached.

"I think we got 'em all," Jenkins said with a weary smile.

"I hope so," Reginald replied as he put two rounds into the grave and ended the girl's suffering for good. "Do the bodies. Clean the area. We're out in twenty."

Kloss, the team's gun smith, walked over with an oversized canteen.

Reginald fought back a hungry smile as the human tossed it his way. The divorced vampire hunter caught it, unscrewed the top, and drank back three pints of chilled blood. Its sweet power raced through his undead frame. Better than sex, booze, or anything else, it made him shudder with ecstasy.

As he fed, Reginald's mind went back to that awful June night in Vegas. He had just drunkenly stumbled out of his favorite bar when he heard a cry for help in an adjacent alley. Curious, he found a damned-fine blonde lying in a pool of her own blood.

She had been shot up pretty badly. When Reginald got too close, fangs slid out as she got up and rushed him. The wounded vampire bit into the left side of his neck and began to withdraw his lifeblood with disturbing efficiency. Even though she was stronger than Reginald, he wasn't in the mood to die that night.

Even with her fangs in his neck, Reginald pulled a cheap pen out of his pocket and started stabbing her. He opened up left carotid artery, her left eardrum, and even her left boob. The vampire screamed as she staggered away from him. Reginald used the opening to grab a discarded wooden mop.

He savagely broke it across the top of her skull. As she went down, he then staked her with its broken edge. The good news was that the vampire died on the spot. The bad news was that, seconds later, Reginald hit the ground and convulsed as her bite—coupled with massive blood loss—began to kill him. Since he still had some blood left in him, he began to turn.

Then a crew of vampire hunters came along.

The six-person team had just ambushed a nest of vampires. The wounded lady vamp had barely escaped the one-sided slaughter, only to get dropped by a lucky drunk. Two of the hunters hacked up her corpse (a standard precaution). The other four debated on whether or not to kill Reginald.

Standard procedure was also to kill anyone—even a fellow team member—after a vampire bite. Reginald's case, however, was unique. With this nest of vampires taken out, there was no psychic link to influence his mind. Plus, anyone who could kill a vampire with a pen and a broken mop handle could be of use.

They decided to take him into custody and contacted Rome for instructions.

After a month of training, Reginald made his official debut as a vampire hunter. The arrangement was simple: he'd find vampire nests and his backup team(s) would put them down. His incisors/fangs were surgically-removed and replaced with fake teeth. Without them, he couldn't spawn. Reginald would be fed fresh blood, laced with a specially-designed, difficult-to-replicate narcotic poison. It actually made Reginald stronger and faster than others of his kind. If he ever went rogue, they'd cut off his blood supply. Reginald called the concoction his "Leash" because of the side effects. The amplified withdrawal would hit him in roughly a day. Regular human blood wouldn't take the edge off, nor would any other kind of drug. Without the Leash, he'd be weaker than a ninety-pound human in a matter of days, afflicted by constant pain. Reginald was assured that he'd die in a week without (at least) one dose.

As he was supposed to be dead anyway, Reginald didn't mind.

His fellow hunters saw to it that he was fed three "meals" a day—and not just because they liked him. He was their best hunter. Vampire nests learned to cover their tracks very well. Usually, hunt teams spent weeks tracking a nest before they could pin it down. Reginald could simply go out at night and catch a psychic "whiff" of a nest's link.

Then he'd get close enough for his nose to get a vampire's actual scent. Once he found the vamp, he'd follow the target(s) to the nest and then call in a strike. Every so often, he and his fellow hunters would actually show up in time to save an innocent life or two.

To the outside world, Reginald was currently being sought for a cross-country murder spree. They didn't have his name or description (yet). But his M.O. involved beheading victims (vampires) and stealing anything of value that they might have. While the

Vatican didn't directly pay him or even offer him dental, they supplied him with tactical assistance.

He had access to safe houses, petty fences to process his stolen merchandise, and plenty of wooden hollow points. Without their aid, the FBI would've caught up to him by now. Of course, if he ever ended up behind bars, Reginald knew that Rome would get him out somehow—as long as he behaved. That's why he wouldn't mind asking them to pay his child support bill. The money wasn't going to him and Rome certainly had the cash to cover the expense.

Reginald finished feeding and capped the canteen. Menschel, the team's communications geek, handed him a new (red) burner phone. He would've overheard any calls made on it.

"Your ex sounds like a real bitch," he joked as Reginald unplugged his ear phones and slipped them into the new phone.

"Yeah," Reginald sadly replied as he tossed his old phone into the fire. "They're like that in Vegas. Wouldn't have 'em any other way."

INSTRUCTIONS

I drove up to Andy's loft after a solid week of unreturned voice messages. Things weren't right since our last date. Usually, he was attentive and funny. Not to mention horny. In the two years we dated, last week's dinner/movie outing was the first time he didn't get frisky with me.

Andy looked sad, wouldn't tell me what was wrong, and threw out plenty of other signals which told me that a break-up was in the works. Maybe he was dumping me for another chick. Or maybe he was just breaking up with me. Either way, I've been dumped enough times to recognize the warning signs.

What doesn't make sense is why he'd break up with me now.

Everything, up to that date, was picture-book perfect: except for the fact that he hadn't put a ring on me yet. Our last argument was three months ago, when he talked me out of meeting his parents (yet again). I forced myself not to rock the boat because guys like him didn't fall out of the sky.

Andy could play six instruments, spoke five languages, and made solid money as a research expert. He was also handsome, great in bed, good with kids, and patient with my mood swings. Aside from some mild snoring and poor taste in movies, he'd make the perfect husband. I wasn't going to lose him without a fight.

As I pulled up, I saw a plain white moving truck in front of his place. Two bulky, uniformed movers were toting Andy's red couch out of the front door and loading it into the truck. Andy followed them out with a cell phone at his ear. Well fuck me silly! He was leaving town!

I jaywalked with a pissed-off expression. A car swerved around me and honked. I didn't take my eyes off him as I reached the curb.

"You're moving?!"

The movers exchanged amused smiles as they loaded the couch into the truck. Andy turned around, surprised to see me.

"Uh, Lana, I wanted—"

I snatched the phone from his hand and tossed it into the truck.

"Why didn't you tell me?!"

"I wanted to," Andy began. "But it's . . . complicated."

I folded my arms and assumed my "stubborn" stance. He knew it well.

"Spell it out for me then, sweetheart."

"I have to leave the country."

"For how long?" I asked, shocked by the answer.

"For good."

Andy looked tired, sad, and anxious at the same time.

"Why?"

"You can't tell her," one of the movers said as he stepped off the truck and headed inside. "Orders, remember?"

"Like it matters now?" his partner grinned as he headed passed us too.

I waited for both of them to enter Andy's building.

"Andy, tell me what the hell is going on!"

The love of my life ran a tongue over his perfect lips and pulled a folded gray envelope out of his pocket. Then he pressed it into my hands.

"Follow the instructions perfectly," he told me. "Do it the second you wake up."

"But—"

"Please," Andy insistently whispered. "I'm not supposed to help you at all. But I just can't do it. Please, Lana. Just get in your car and follow those instructions. I'll never see you again. But if you pull this off, you might survive."

"What are you talking about?!"

Andy grabbed me and kissed me with a fiery passion. I tasted a faint hint of cinnamon in that kiss. Then I suddenly got dizzy and started to fall toward the pavement. The last thing I remembered was Andy catching me in his arms and holding me close . . .

I woke up in the middle of his empty loft. I stood up and raced over to the window. The moving truck was gone. A glance at my watch told me I had been down for three hours. Taped to the window was Andy's mysterious envelope. My hands trembled as I opened it up and read its contents.

I'm not a dumb blonde. But I am a dumb brunette.

It took me some time to figure out that the first three pages of numbers—stapled behind the instructions—were account numbers. There was also a note, in Andy's neat cursive. It explained that all 914 of these account numbers were in my name.

According to his instructions, they were worth a combined total of $91,478,084,312.13! I'm a multi-billionaire and probably the richest woman on the planet. How the hell did Andy dump billions of dollars into my hands? And stranger still, why would he? I could barely balance my own checkbook!

As for the instructions, they were pretty simple. I dusted off my passport and rushed to the airport without packing. There was a ticket waiting for me. One long-assed flight later, I ended up in Cairo, Egypt. Once there, I made my way to a port and tracked down a small pleasure ship called *The Aeneas*.

The boat was owned by Chad Young. A twenty-something friend of Andy's, Chad was given instructions to steal his rich dad's boat and sail here. The kid was equally clueless about what was going on but he was good company—and cute too.

I waited on the boat while he wrangled up some fresh supplies. Then we sailed deep into the Atlantic and weighed anchor. We waited three hours, per Andy's instructions, before a rusty old submarine surfaced next to the yacht. Out popped a bunch of French smugglers who greeted us with smiles and decent wine.

They were led by "Captain" Renard Dupreon. He too knew Andy and welcomed us board. We were the last of a string of pickups, all arranged by my ex-boyfriend. There were about fifty passengers and crew crammed into a stolen Russian sub built during the early 70's.

The crew set a course for the Horn of Africa. While everyone gossiped about what was going on, Dupreon seemed to be in the know. The passengers were all experts in something—from computers to agriculture to medical science. On the second night, while Dupreon and I were playing a drinking game in his private quarters, he let his guard down.

"I'm not from here," Dupreon told me over a glass of white wine.

"Me neither," I half-drunkenly giggled. "I'm from Pasadena."

"No," replied the Frenchman. "I'm not from this Earth. I'm from another one."

"Huh?"

"There are other Earths out there," Dupreon replied with a careless wave of his right hand. "We figured out how to travel between them. Andy and I were assigned to do a survey mission to this world."

"Why'd you come here? Surely your world's more advanced."

"True," Dupreon nodded as he finished his wine and poured himself another. "But our interests are more sociological and cultural. We like to know how your world differs from ours."

I pointed to my empty glass. "For example?"

Dupreon shrugged as he refilled my glass.

"That, eh, fellow with the symbol for a name . . . Prince, is it? He's a singer on your world, right?"

I nodded.

"On my Earth, he's a retired basketball star. He and Michael Jordan took the Golden State Warriors to three NBA World Championships."

"No way!" I exclaimed as I eyed his body language. He wasn't lying. I work at a salon, so I should know.

"It's true," Dupreon replied. "We study the subtle nuances of history, politics, art—all of it. We've studied Earths like yours for centuries—worlds where the Roman Empire didn't fall or where Islam never took root. Quite fascinating outcomes."

"So, why did Andy leave?"

"He was reassigned to another Earth. They wanted him there before this world's next Ice Age begins."

I was too stunned to reply as Dupreon leaned over his small desk and peered at a calendar with his beady little eyes.

"NASA should spot the asteroid in another week or so. Two weeks after that, it'll plow through your atmosphere. Once it hits, think nuclear winter and the end of most life on this planet."

"Waitaminute! Wouldn't NASA's telescopes spot it years in advance?"

"Normally," Dupreon nodded. "Too bad your NASA geniuses never spotted the wormhole sitting between the moon and Mars. By our calculations, a huge chunk of long-exploded planet will plunge through that wormhole and crash straight into the Canadian Rockies."

"Couldn't someone shoot it down with a nuke?"

"It's a bit smaller than my native France," he sadly replied. "Your missiles can't stop it. And while we have the technology to intervene, our rules explicitly prevent us from doing so."

"Why the hell not?! You could save billions of lives!"

Dupreon gave me a rueful sigh.

"My superiors have never before studied an Earth right after an asteroid hit. They'd like to know which species survive and how the remnants of humanity—if any—endure this catastrophe. That's why I'm still here. We estimated that the only safe land mass is deep in the Congo, of all places. I'll rendezvous nearby with other members of my survey team and catalog the damage. Oddly enough, there's nothing in the rules that says we can't take hitchhikers with us."

"And so here we are?" I asked as I downed my glass and held it out.

"*Oui*," Dupreon nodded as he refilled my glass. "I'll drop you and my other passengers off and dock at an undersea bunker to ride out the impact. Make your way to the Congo with the money Andrew gave you. I'd suggest you do some massive shopping and surround yourself with manpower and resources. Once civilization falls, that windfall he left you won't amount to much. Still, you'll be in an interesting position."

"What kind of position?"

"Well my dear," Dupreon replied as he raised his glass to me. "Andy figured that you should rule the world. Everyone on this boat's pretty much on the same page. In exchange for being saved from certain death, they're to follow your lead and help you rebuild human civilization."

I paused, utterly dumbfounded by the fact that Andy was handing me the keys to the world.

"Why me?! I don't want to rule the fucking world!"

"Good," Dupreon winked. "A worthy leader shouldn't want the job. It sucks. And your obvious goal should be to help the human race survive the difficult times to come. Andy figured you'd be more than qualified."

"Why?! I'm no world leader!"

Dupreon paused and drunkenly giggled. I waited for him to get back to the point.

"On my Earth, you're a three-star general: the youngest in the history of the U.S. Army. She saw combat on four continents and earned more medals than any other soldier in American history . . . again, on my world. Andy figured that if your dimensional counterpart was bright enough to accomplish all that, then surely you're the right person to save the human race on this world. It's an interesting theory. One worthy of testing, no?"

I paused for a moment and let Dupreon's words sink in.

"No wonder he wanted to fuck me!"

Dupreon laughed himself into tears. I shook my head in quiet disbelief and wished that I had something stronger to gulp down right now. Instead, I finished off my wine and held up my glass.

"So...tell me more about my other self."

DUTY CALLS

I ejected the mag and slipped in my last one. My pain tolerance was shot. The blurred vision implied massive blood loss. While I wasn't afraid of my situation, I didn't dare look down. Slumped against someone else's tombstone, I knew that if I looked down, my brain would realize that I was dying . . . and that would be that.

Dying could come later. A few minutes from now would be just fine. Joe needed me, which was why I stepped into the pain and rose to my feet with shaky hands and wobbly feet. I heard more gunshots ring off in the distant, fog-shrouded night.

I stepped over my kills and stubbornly headed toward my only friend. Joe was the one person in this world who believed in me. Who understood my sins and why I did what I did for God and country. A sense of duty was hard to keep these days. After the Towers fell, I stepped up and became a Marine. My soft morals and impressive wits earned me a fast-track into black ops, where I became something of a household name.

Didn't want to kill so many people. Some of them could've been spared. The sad thing about the Middle East was that anyone not in diapers was a threat. Then again, I've killed babies too—just for being in the wrong place at the wrong time. Had I stayed in college and gotten that MBA, I'd probably be some cold-hearted corporate prick with a wife, two kids, and a mistress. Instead, I've helped topple governments.

Somewhere along the line, Uncle Sam wrote me off.

A new administration with a more humane foreign policy. Some suit looked over my file and ratted me out.

They came to lock me up and I let 'em. I wasn't a monster. I was a patriot. I told them to reactivate me when they needed me. My confidence scared them but we both knew the day would come. Six weeks in the hole, an op came up. Flat-out suicide mission. Someone needed to go into Iran and extract a priest who was arrested for espionage. As it turned out, this priest really was a spy and had vital secrets in his head. I gave them a grocery list of op tech and asked for backup. The op tech was denied and instead of a team, they gave me Joe Weddles.

Unlike me, Joe had a conscience. Ten years my senior, he was a half-drunk washout with tons of contacts, field experience, and something of a death wish. Someone paired us together thinking that both of us (and the priest) would die in a botched rescue attempt. If those secrets died with the priest, the pricks in Washington wouldn't mind.

We went in, sized up the situation, and then poisoned the priest. After his "death," we swapped him out for a double. Apparently, Joe had a taxidermist friend who dabbled in post-mortem plastic surgery. When the rescue came to light, Tehran was furious. Langley was awed.

Washington made our partnership permanent after that incident. A functional madman and a dysfunctional alcoholic. We did the suicidal ops and impossible missions, usually having to steal the funds to pull them off. It was a fun learning experience. Joe was the brains. I was the talent. We had a 41.7% success rate, which was near-miraculous.

Could've gone on for years . . . except it didn't.

Someone leaked us out (again). This time, a kill team was waiting at my loft. American and well-trained, they almost got me. I got them back. Took their gear and weapons. Rather than patch myself up, I pinged

Joe's cell phone and raced over to save him. Tactical sense told me to leave him behind. My sense of duty refused to listen. So here I was, dying in bloody droplets, fairly certain that Joe was already dead. As it turned out, I walked into the aftermath of a capture. Joe was on his stomach, getting flex cuffed. For some reason, they wanted him alive. While my attackers were dressed in heavy tactical gear, Joe's foes were in civilian dress. Four of them were dead. A fifth pinned Joe to the ground. The last one was calling for extraction when I put two rounds through her head. The guy cuffing Joe gawked up at me as he went for his gun. I dropped him and—

—fell down.

"Get ghost," I managed to wheeze.

Joe swallowed hard.

When we paired up, I avoided the mistakes of his past handlers. Rather than trying to get him off the bottle, I forced him to work out. The balding, potbellied agent lost thirty pounds and picked up twenty back in muscle. He quit smoking, used mild steroids, and limited his drinking to the expensive stuff. Made a new man out of him. Proof of that was the way he produced a blade out of nowhere and deftly cut himself loose.

Joe grabbed a flashlight from the dead woman and rushed over to me.

"Goddamn it, Neil!" Joe gasped, checking my wounds.

I didn't need to look. My brain knew it was fucked and was sending me "pain cards" as a sign of its displeasure. Breathing was getting harder.

"End me and run," I told him.

We both had escape plans and enough stolen assets to disappear for life. If Joe kept his wits, he'd be fine. I handed my gun to Joe. He placed it between my eyes with tons of regret in his eyes and a steady hand. I took pride in that steady hand, which used to shake when we met. He was a better agent because of me, better able to live with his flaws. At least I left one positive mark in the world.

"Forgive me," Joe whispered before pulling the trigger.

Tears formed in his eyes as Joe pulled an earpiece out of his jacket. The four "kills" he had taken out began to stir. They were playing possum?! The staged kill zone was good enough to fool my wearied ass.

"The chapter is closed," Joe reported. "Say again, the chapter is closed."

That was our jargon for a successful kill. Joe wasn't the target—just me. I lay there, shaking my head, as vans rolled up in the distance. A clean-up crew arrived, along with a support team of shooters, and Gerald Bialchi. The fat suit was two tiers above our handler. He hated us both but couldn't knock our results.

Someone zipped me up in a body bag and carried me off. Bialchi walked over with a silver flask and offered it to Neil, who regarded the fifty-something like the slime he was. Bialchi wanted Neil to fall off the wagon again. Instead, Neil declined the flask. He liked who he was just fine. Besides, knowing Bialchi, the flask might've been laced.

"Congratulations, Joe," said Bialchi. "You're out of the shit house."

I got up and walked over to them. At some point, I'd have to wonder why I wasn't in Hell. I was fully expecting to go there when I died. Made more sense than Heaven. Guess I hadn't lost my flair for the impossible.

"You didn't have to write him off," Joe scowled.

"We needed him gone, Neil," Bialchi explained. "The Oversight investigation's a nail in the program's coffin. You were deemed salvageable. Be grateful and move on."

"So what now?"

"You go before the Hill and lie," Bialchi shrugged. "Do it well enough and you'll get a nice, safe desk to age behind, with a guaranteed pension. You'll never have to pull a trigger again."

Joe shook his head and pointed at the meat wagon. "I meant with Neil. For all he's done, the kid deserves a slot in Arlington."

Bialchi shook his head. "The man's got a date with an acid bath. He needs to disappear, Joe. Simple as that."

The fat fuck took a swig from the flask and walked off. He made it four paces before I killed him. An unarmed man of my talents could kill three Bialchis in about four seconds. Being a ghost and all, I stuck with the basics. I grabbed him around the throat with both hands and choked the fucking life out of him.

"I need some help over here!" Joe yelled as Bialchi dropped the flask and grabbed through my intangible spectral hands.

Eyes bulging, all Bialchi could do was die. I forced him to the ground with Joe shouting for help. Some of his people rushed over with a first aid kit and tried to revive Bialchi. Two of them pulled Joe back and flex cuffed him again, thinking he had something to do with it. My former partner's protests were fun to hear as I removed my hands from Bialchi's throat.

They were mystified by the bruise marks. Walking past a gawking sentry, I admired his silenced UMP-45. Maybe that's why I cracked him in the windpipe and snatched it away as he died. They gawked at the floating gun before I mowed them down—sparing only Joe.

As I pressed the hot barrel against his face, my ex-partner's pained expression faded into realization, relief, and then a quiet acceptance. "'I don't know but I've been told,'" Joe chanted. "'Good Marines, they don't grow old.'" "Not funny," I growled. "You sold me out, you piece of shit! Why?!" Joe looked up at the UMP-45, waiting to die. "Answer me!" He didn't. It took me a while to remember that he couldn't. I was a ghost. People aren't supposed to see ghosts. With a sigh, I killed my only friend and stood up. Answers . . . I needed answers.

Stumped, I dropped the SMG, walked out of the cemetery, and crossed the street. People and vehicles passed through me. I spotted an empty restaurant and went inside. Apparently, the raging gun battle had cleared out the place. Police were cordoning the area off while federal trench coats kept everyone out of the cemetery.

I headed for the men's room and looked at myself in the mirror for several minutes. Pleased to have a fucking reflection, I leaned up against the sink and took in my transparent form. My bland expression, balding head, trimmed blonde beard, and a corpse-like pallor. I still wore the bullet-riddled Kevlar vest I had died in, along with the combat harness and assorted op tech loaded on it. My t-shirt and jeans were shot up too.

Yet there wasn't a mark on me. Over my head was something I didn't expect to see—a fiery halo. Maybe Heaven wasn't a place but a status. Whatever my reason for still being here, I'd just have to roll with it. Then the broad strokes of a plan came to mind.

Joe and I still had assets in the field. Granted, Bialchi would've emptied our accounts and stashes but those could be replaced. Once I handled the money problem, I'd have to recruit new assets—including someone in Langley. Since I was fucking invisible, I'd have to do it all by e-mail. My assets would find the trouble and I'd go and settle it—at least, until I could afford the muscle to do it for me.

In essence, I'd be creating a phantom spy network. Someone or some group would eventually come along and shut me down. I'd have to plan for that. A sad grin crossed my face as I remembered all of the tricks Joe had taught me. Guess our partnership had been mutually beneficial.

That's the thing about duty. Joe and I used to joke that it was a four-letter word that would kill us both someday. Clearly, it had (and then some). The thing was, I couldn't walk away from it.

Even in death, I just couldn't walk away.

EL GRINGO CANTINA

Broadstrike raced over the clouds at a leisurely speed of MACH 2. In his early 30's, the thickly-muscled villain's black-and-red costume clung as a second skin. His matching boots and cape both had a snarling skull emblem. While he also wore a red mask, it only covered the upper part of his brutish, malevolent face. Like the rest of him, Broadstrike's dark-blue buzz cut seemed unaffected by the high-speed travel. Intense, blue eyes glared through the light cloud cover and toward the rapidly-approaching coastline of Belize. A GPS tracking device in his right glove beeped. Broadstrike abruptly came to a hovering stop, roughly a half-kilometer up. His enhanced vision easily spotted a cluster of lights and a swath of sunny beach below.

He grinned and streaked downward.

Mr. Impossible was hiding out here in a bar called the *El Gringo Cantina*. Broadstrike couldn't wait to find out if months of searching would finally turn up his arch nemesis—the only man alive who had ever beaten him in one-on-one combat. After the eighteen-hour slugfest, Mr. Impossible had personally delivered him to the Shell—a high-security prison for superhuman criminals. It took Broadstrike four-and-three-quarter years to escape. Upon doing so, Broadstrike was informed that Mr. Impossible had "hung up his cape."

The hero's departure had been quite a blow to the good guys—especially in Civiticus. Under Mr. Impossible's protection, the glass-and-steel metropolis used to be the safest city in America. Now, it was ranked as one of the most dangerous. Some of the lesser villains were even afraid to live there.

Why had the world's greatest super hero mysteriously vanished? The rumors varied. Some said he found true love. Others claimed he was dead and no one wanted to admit it. He even heard a rumor that Mr. Impossible had decided to switch sides and became a criminal.

All of the rumors were wrong—not that he cared. Broadstrike landed on both feet with a thunderous boom. Sand flew in all directions. The locals ran away as Broadstrike stood at the center of a massive impact crater. The villain turned around and strode out of it. His ire-filled eyes narrowed upon a glowing neon sign for *El Gringo Cantina*. Fists clenched, he moved forward with vengeance in his blood.

He would call out Mr. Impossible and then break the hero's bones—one for each month spent locked away in the Shell. Broadstrike passed through the cantina's saloon-style double doors and let them swing behind him. He counted ten frightened Belizean locals, three elderly white tourists, and a middle-aged white man behind the bar.

A soccer game was on a corner-mounted TV, just over the bartender's right shoulder. Unlike the other patrons, the bartender regarded Broadstrike like just another customer. Then the man belched and poured himself a mug of beer. The villain walked over to the bar and intently studied the gray-eyed, forty-something bartender. He stood about 5'7", weighed a bit over 180 pounds with shoulder-length, salt-and-pepper hair.

The aging pretty boy struck Broadstrike as . . . familiar.

"Heya Broadstrike," the bartender said with a friendly nod. "What are you drinking?"

While the bar patrons abruptly ran for the door, Broadstrike sat on a stool.

"Nothing, thanks," replied the villain.

The bartender shrugged, gave Broadstrike a slight toast, and then turned his back. The super villain looked around the deserted cantina as the bartender eyed the soccer game.

"How do you know me?" Broadstrike asked.

"I kicked your ass about what . . . five years ago?" shrugged the bartender.

Broadstrike's face twisted with shock, recognition, and then outright laughter as he jumped to his feet. Five years ago, Mr. Impossible was 6'7" and built like a pagan god of strength. He could fly at MACH 9, lift cruise liners with ease, and once survived a point-blank nuke blast. Now, he was a scrawny little bartender! After the first twenty seconds of Broadstrike's non-stop laughter, Mr. Impossible gave him a half-glance.

"What's so funny?"

"You're a wuss now!" Broadstrike exclaimed with a reddening face, tears forming in his eyes. "I came all this way to break you in half and you're an Average Joe!"

"Well," Mr. Impossible sipped his beer with a shrug. "That's life. Two years back, I started losing my powers. Couldn't fly as fast. My kinetic force beams didn't zap as hard. Then I started to shrink. I decided to call it quits before some lucky purse snatcher ended me."

Broadstrike needed a few seconds to catch his breath. The escaped villain then paused to wipe his eyes as he sat down again. Mr. Impossible glanced back at the TV, only to sigh as the game went to a *Viagra* commercial.

"How'd you lose your powers?" asked the villain.

"I dunno," Mr. Impossible replied as he turned back toward Broadstrike. "I tried to undo it but couldn't."

"You could've hidden yourself better."

"Not really," Mr. Impossible countered as he leaned against the bar and set his mug down. "I get to watch scantily-clad women come and go. The bar's a joy to run. I even get to work on my surfing. No sir, there's no better place than here."

"How come no one's snuffed you by now?"

"You think you're the first bad guy to find me?" Mr. Impossible chuckled. "Don't flatter yourself."

"How many?"

Mr. Impossible glanced up at the ceiling.

"You're actually the . . . ninth (?) super villain to track me down. They all wanted me dead—some more than you."

"What happened to the other eight?"

Mr. Impossible gave his former adversary a smug grin.

"Sharks gotta eat, too."

Broadstrike regarded his former enemy with obvious skepticism.

"You took out eight super villains . . . without your powers? How?"

"Try me and find out," the ex-hero teased as he picked up his mug.

"You couldn't survive a sneeze from me, old man," Broadstrike growled. "Don't push your luck."

The classic difference between heroes and villains was that villains talked too damned much. Had Mr. Impossible been a bad guy, he might've gloated that Broadstrike's powers were (temporarily) negated the second he entered the bar. That he was wearing a fast-acting forcefield rig under his apron. Or that no fewer than fifty concealed weapons were locked on to Broadstrike's exposed skull—ready to fire.

"Call me Huey," said the bartender.

"Huh?"

"Huey Slyne. That's my name now."

"Why are you still alive? I know it's not luck."

"You're right," Huey nodded. "The answer's pretty simple: think of the bad guys I've locked away. Some were brutes like you. Others were mad scientist types who couldn't bench-press 100 pounds . . . but were way smarter than me. Whenever I took down an evil genius, I kept any schematics I could find. Sometimes, I even snagged a device or two—especially anything capable of knocking me around in my prime."

The bartender allowed himself a brief moment of self-pity.

"Sure enough, that day has come and gone."

Broadstrike couldn't believe his ears. This was the same guy who had saved the world countless times and defeated adversaries too numerous to mention. He suddenly found it all so depressing.

"So that's it? You're just gonna grow old and bang anything in a thong?"

"Don't knock it," Huey grinned.

"What about Civiticus?" asked Broadstrike.

"Not my problem anymore," Huey replied. "Someone else can take over."

"I passed through there a few weeks ago," Broadstrike said with a disgusted shake of his head. "Heroes stay the hell away. Guess your shoes were too big to fill."

"That's too bad," Huey shrugged as he let loose an impressive belch and picked up his beer. "But it's not my fight anymore, kid."

Broadstrike saw a bowl of shelled pistachios and helped himself to a handful.

"The better question is: What are you gonna do now?" Huey asked as he finished his beer.

"I suppose I'll find some mastermind with deep pockets and be his chief enforcer."

Huey gave his former adversary an agreeable nod.

"I'm sure you'll enjoy that."

To be honest, Broadstrike wouldn't. While the Shell was an ultramax prison for supers, it also doubled as a networking hub for villains. Most of his fellow convicts hustled to get well-paying "evil minion" gigs when they got out. Personally, he liked running solo and beating down anyone in his path. Before prison, he only teamed up with like-minded villains of his high caliber. Broadstrike stole, wrecked, and did whatever he wanted. Working for some arrogant prick—especially a plain old human—just didn't appeal. Sadly, he wasn't up for his pre-prison, highly-chaotic lifestyle either. Four-plus years in prison had aged his soul a bit.

"What do you think I should do?" Broadstrike impulsively asked.

Huey faked his surprise at the question.

"What do I think?"

Huey shrugged and pretended to think it over for a moment as he refilled his glass halfway.

"Why not take my place?"

Broadstrike started to laugh at the notion . . . only to stop.

It would be an interesting challenge, even though he'd still be broke. Being a super hero rarely paid anything unless said hero worked for someone, which (again) wasn't his style. Plus, he was also an escaped felon.

Huey studied Broadstrike's conflicted reaction. Then he did some quick math. With a sigh, the former hero reached under the bar and tossed Broadstrike a red velvet bag. The villain opened it up to find a sizeable pile of diamonds inside.

"When I busted up an operation, I'd (sometimes) skim some of the profits: strictly for a rainy day, you understand."

Broadstrike eyed his former enemy with renewed respect.

"How much are these worth?"

"In today's market? Beats me," Huey admitted. "But it should cover your start-up costs. I could point you to a few vacant lairs in Civiticus. If you were to save said shithole from its criminal element, I could even call in a few favors and get you pardoned."

"You'd do that?"

"Why not? Just return the favor by occasionally saving the world—with me on it."

"I'd make a lot of enemies . . ." Broadstrike mused aloud.

The only thing super villains hated more than super heroes were fellow villains who "sold out" and became super heroes themselves.

"But you'd also get into a lot more interesting fights, now wouldn't you? Not to mention the fame, adoration, and swarms of hot women trying to rip off your tights."

"Really?" Broadstrike asked.

Since his escape, he hadn't bothered getting laid. His desire for vengeance had been too strong.

"I could tell you some interesting stories," Huey chuckled.

Broadstrike tucked the diamonds into a belt pouch and eyed the beer taps.

"Maybe I could use a beer after all."

THE NEW ME

Gil Rice blandly whistled to himself as he showered in the hotel bathroom. The raven-haired fellow was in his late thirties, with an average height and fair skin. He had a boyishly-handsome face that didn't go very well with his chubby frame—an unfortunate side-effect of his fiancée's fine cooking.

He wrapped a white towel around his waist and stepped out onto the bathroom floor. Gil checked himself out in the mirror before reaching for one of the other half-dozen white towels that were stacked over the toilet. As he dried his graying black hair, Gil grinned to himself, pleased that he could finally set the wedding date. Fully aware of Stacy's growing impatience, he wanted to tie a few loose ends down.

She could only see as far as the honeymoon. Being a financial planner, Gil was already arranging their retirement savings and setting up enough trust fund money for three kids. He had meticulously scrimped, saved, and wisely invested over their seven-year relationship. Now, it was paying off. All he had to do was get back to her.

Gil planned to check out, attend the last day of this tedious convention, and then fly home. Stacy would pick Gil up from the airport. He'd tell her about the large cathedral wedding he had planned and the exact date he had in mind. Maybe she'd even be happy enough to kick out the "good sex" . . . the kind that actually lasted a while. All in all, it should be a very good night indeed.

There was a knock on the door.

Curious, Gil draped the second towel around his neck, left the bathroom, and answered it without looking through the spy hole. In the doorway stood a scowling copy of himself! The double had the same face, height, and gut as Gil. He even had two white towels wrapped around him the same way.

But there were differences as well. For one thing, the real Gil had natural color to him: slightly-tanned skin, gray eyes, red lips, et cetera. His duplicate looked as if he stepped out of an old black-and-white movie screen. The lack of real color was eerie (from his white skin to his jet-black eyes).

"Hello," his wet double said with an eerie smile. "Sorry I didn't call first."

Gil started to respond when his double sucker-punched him in the gut. The double shoved Gil further into the room before slamming the door shut.

"You're probably wondering what the hell is going on, right?"

Wheezing from the gut punch, Gil backed away and looked for someplace to run. He couldn't get to the bathroom and they were on the twelfth floor. The only way out was through.

"Who are you?" Gil asked between coughs.

"I'm you . . . as you're supposed to be."

"Supposed to be?" Gil asked.

The double cracked his knuckles and slowly advanced. Gil, on the other hand, kept backing away. He wished he had a gun, an axe, or anything that could help him fight his way past this lunatic. The only potential "weapons" within easy reach were the towel around his neck and his portable alarm clock on a nearby table.

"I've been sent here to replace you."

"Why would anyone want to replace me?!"

"Not anyone, Gil. God sent me."

Gil curiously cocked his head as his double began to pace.

"Excuse me?"

The double pulled a bottle of cologne from Gil's overnight bag, opened it, and sniffed the cap approvingly.

"God sent me to take over your life because you're living it all wrong."

"I don't follow," Gil replied, as a bad idea occurred to him.

"Contrary to biblical belief, mankind does not have free will. Every living being, down to the lowest microbe, has a particular role to play in God's grand design. Period. Poofka. Without exception. But, like in every complex machine, the occasional 'glitch' occurs. In this case, the glitch is you."

"What are you saying?" Gil asked. "That I have free will?"

The double disapprovingly nodded.

"Basically? Yeah, you're fucking up the program. When this happens, God personally makes a duplicate of the offending party."

"What happens to me?" Gil asked.

"I kill you, take over, and your life goes downhill."

"What? My life's supposed to suck?"

With a knowing chuckle, the double closed the cologne bottle, dropped it back into the bag, and sat on the corner of the bed.

"Let me put it this way—you're supposed to be on a multi-state killing spree. I mean, right now, as we speak. Instead, you're toweling off your fat ass and making wedding plans for your incredibly boring fiancée, who was supposed to be Victim #16."

Gil didn't want to believe his double's words . . . . yet he found himself oddly convinced. He'd grown up in an abusive household, which left him with a dark side—one which twisted the way he saw the world.

"I'm not a psycho," Gil quietly argued, his face turning red.

"Of course you are," the double said with a shake of his head. "Don't lie to yourself, Gil. You stopped your 'inner madman' every time you refused to look at a beautiful co-ed or shied away from people you instinctively knew would ignite the killing rage in you. You're a T-Rex in sheep's clothing, my friend. Time to roar."

"But that's not possible!" Gil countered stubbornly. "I love Stacy!"

"Do you?" Gil's double mockingly grinned. "It's fair to say that you only allowed yourself to get close to Stacy because she's incapable of pissing off anybody with that cotton candy attitude of hers. Hell, you haven't had one good fight in the seven years you've been dating! She's like Marge Simpson—but without all the blue hair."

For some reason, as he confronted his evil self, Gil's fear went away. In its place sparked that dark side. Instead of forcing it down (yet again), he let it loose. Gil's fingers clenched into fists as he stared his double dead in the eye.

"What happens if I kill you?" Gil asked with a cold tone.

The double looked up at the ceiling and laughed . . . until Gil snatched up the alarm clock and smashed it across the double's face.

The double grunted as he staggered back with a black-bloodied jaw. Gil dropped the clock and rushed in with a series of wild punches. His double shrugged off the first and second swings but staggered on the third. Then Gil kicked his double in the balls. His waist towel fell off as he tackled the naked imposter to the floor. Gil's fists rose and fell as he beat his double's face to a bloody pulp.

Gil swung until he was too tired to swing anymore . . . then he checked the corpse for a pulse. The newly-minted killer slowed his breathing as he got up and staggered toward his phone to call 911. Then Gil paused. How would he explain the dead copy of himself? Or that God sent a double to kill him?

Gil put the phone down and turned around—
—and found himself alone in the room.

There wasn't a corpse or signs of a struggle. The alarm clock was on the table, completely undamaged. His towels were around his neck and waist. Gil shook his head and went into the bathroom, wondering if he had lost his damned mind. He ran some cold water and was about splash some on his face when he looked into the mirror. The image froze him in place.

Gil had blood splattered across his face.

And it was black.

THE GIZMO SLEUTH

I watched Baron Helmut von Vindischein rant into
the microphone below. The short, bald Nazi madman
wore his standard white uniform, which strangely made
him resemble a malicious orthodontist. His audience, a
battalion of elite Nazi shock troopers, was absolutely
enraptured by his speech. Above their impromptu rally,
I crept along in a stolen sergeant's uniform. My target
was ahead—a really large rocket aimed at Washington,
D.C.

What got my mind to spinning was that we were in
the Baron's mountain castle, somewhere in Germany . . .
thousands of miles away! The mad scientist in me
wanted to ask Vindischein how he had managed to build
what he referred to as an "Intercontinental Ballistic
Rocket"—or "IBR" for short. Unfortunately,
Vindischein had tried to kill me so many times this week
that I doubt he'd ever tell me.

Two guards stood in my path but my stolen uniform
outranked theirs. The young men saluted me perfectly,
their faces eager as they listened to Vindischein's vow to
destroy America's political core in one swift stroke.
Then, the baron went on to explain how his teleportation
gates would send elite battalions—like the one in this
castle—from different staging points in Germany to the
heart of every other major American city. Backed up by
tanks and artillery, they'd launch a second Blitzkrieg.
Vindischein estimated that they'd conquer the United
States inside of a week. And once the Americans fell . .
. I'd heard enough.

Time to move.

"Is everything secure?" I asked the guards in fluent
German, courtesy of my Linguisto-Watch. As long as I

possessed the watch, I could speak the tongue better than I could my own.

"Yessir," they almost said in unison.

"Good," I smiled as I clocked the leftmost soldier with a hard right to the jaw. As he fell to the catwalk, the soldier on the right tried to shoot me. My knee to his groin was just a bit faster. I snatched his machine gun and nailed him in the gut with the butt end of it. Then, more on instinct, I pitched him over the side . . . which probably wasn't a good idea. The poor kid screamed like a little girl all the way down and landed smack-dab into the middle of the troop assembly.

Vindischein glared up at me through his monocle and yelled for his troops—most of them armed—to kill me. They raised their pistols, rifles, and machine guns as spotlights swiveled toward my position. I felt like skeet as bullets flew my way. Luckily, I still had the Compresso-Pack on my back. While it resembled a harmless olive-drab backpack, it was essentially an eight-pound gizmo warehouse. Before this mission, I had stuffed most of my own gadgetry inside of it. While they weren't as impressive as Vindischein's devices, they had gotten my sorry hide this far.

I ducked low, reached into the Compresso-Pack, and pulled out a handful of Chaos Pellets. I tossed them over the side as I ran. Their satisfying little pops sounded off as they hit the floor below and released my homemade brew of delirium-inducing chemicals. I grinned as the bluish mist rapidly spread among the soldiers below. In a few seconds, the poor bastards wouldn't know which way was up. The few shots which continued seemed to go in all directions.

I reached the IBR and marveled at its eight hundred feet of majestic height. Then, I realized that blowing it up just wouldn't be right. There might actually be innocent Germans in the vicinity (folks who didn't deserve to be atomized by this 280-megaton weapon). Plus, there was the whole issue of not getting caught in the blast myself.

Frankly, the United States government owed me a paycheck.

That's why I reached into my Compresso-Pack and pulled out an Inflato-Me. Roughly the size and shape of a lunchbox, I pulled the gadget's ripcord and watched it self-inflate into a perfect copy of me in my standard garb—from the brown aviator flight uniform down to the blue scarf I'd normally wear for luck. Luckily, I designed my replicas to be just as smart, too.

"What is your command?" Inflato-Me eagerly asked.

"I need you to disable that rocket behind me— preferably over the ocean—without it exploding."

The Inflato-Me looked over at the rocket and eagerly shifted the weight of the Compresso-Pack on his back. Then we gave each other a thumbs-up gesture and split up. The handsome bastard ran for the rocket. I looked in the opposite direction and saw four clear-headed guards heading my way. I raised the machine gun and mowed them down.

Then I glanced down at Baron Vindischein, who had just finished puking up his breakfast. He pulled out a small black box and extended an antenna from it. Ah! That must be the remote control for the IBR, which would mean. . . aw hell! I ran for my life as the IBR's thrusters fired up. If it launched while I was on this catwalk, I'd end up like an overused fireplace.

I risked a glance over my shoulder and saw that the Inflato-Me had climbed onto the rocket. He was using Magno-Gloves to stick to its metallic hull (just like I would). The weapon of mass damage shook the place as it slowly rose into the air. I pulled out my Grapplo-

Shooter and jumped off the catwalk as the IBR ascended. The catwalk disintegrated as I fired the adhesive grappling hook into a distant rafter and swung over the still-retching Nazi scum.

"Destroy him!" Baron Vindischein yelled as he pointed my way.

I released the Grapplo-Shooter as I landed near a large oak door. I liked oak doors because they always took forever to get through—if you could lock them in time. As luck would have it, this door wasn't locked. A volley of well-aimed shots whizzed past me, which clued me in that my Chaos Pellets were wearing off. A bullet grazed my right arm as I entered a hallway, slammed the oak door closed and bolted it shut.

From my Compresso-Pack, I pulled out a canister of Concrete-In-A-Can and quickly sprayed it around the doorframe. It came out like gray shaving cream and hardened in less than two seconds. Eight seconds later, I heard the first thuds of angry Nazi scum as they began to pound on the door. I resisted the urge to kiss the oak for luck, which was a good thing, seeing as they opted to shoot the door full of holes. While they were expending ammo, I raced for Vindischein's main lab like a white Jesse Owens.

Two days ago, back in Berlin, I found a map of this very castle. I was fortunate enough to commit it to my perfect memory. Without it, I surely would've gotten lost in this maze-like structure. Minutes later, I reached the main lab. It was massive: larger than a third of the castle. But the room looked much smaller on the original map. Then I realized that the lab was designed like my Compress-Pack: basically a massive warehouse fitting into a normal-sized room.

Inside was an array of garish inventions that took my breath away.

He had rows of Inflato-Panzer Tanks, Atomic Shock troopers (complete with little light bulbs on their heads!), and even an armored Rocket Blimp floating near the ceiling. My mouth watered. I wanted to claim the lab in the name of me and try all these neat gadgets out. Then I saw the eighteen teleportation gates—each large enough for a tank to roll through—and came back down from my euphoric state.

I had to tell myself that life and liberty both came before mad science (barely). I told myself a lot of things these days, which wasn't surprising since I'm a mad genius. Unlike Vindischein, I took my Sanity pills on a (mostly) regular basis. Without them, I'd be three times smarter than I am right now . . . but also hopelessly evil. After all, mad genius and morality never mixed.

I sprayed the last of my Concrete-In-A-Can on the room's only two doors (both of which were oak) and knew I had time to kill. I then snatched up a bunch of blueprints for some of his more harmless-looking inventions: a "cellular phone," a "personal video game system," a "VCR", et cetera. From my Compresso-Pack, I pulled a dozen six-packs of my homemade brand of dynamite and tossed them by the main power reactor. The bad guys had reached both doors and were pounding away with a vengeance. They couldn't shoot through, for fear of damaging something volatile in the lab.

Okay then: time for me to go and collect that paycheck.

I ran to the nearest teleportation gate, figured out how it worked, and then set it for the White House lawn. I was a fan of dramatic entrances, after all. I flipped a few switches and the gate flared to life. There was a flash of greenish light and then I could actually see the White House on the other side. Part of me wanted to snatch the schematics for the teleportation gate. Such a fine piece of engineering would be a true shame to destroy. Then I knew how easy it would be for this magnificent technology to be used for nefarious ends. My stolen uniform came with a couple of grenades, so I pulled one. Almost in unison, the wooden doors crashed down. Vindischein personally led the angry charge of Nazis as they closed in on me. I pulled the grenade pin and ran for dear life. Along the way, I threw the grenade toward one of my sticks of dynamite. I needed to be out of this room within the next two seconds. Timing was an issue here. Even if the blast or the angry soldiers didn't kill me, the main lab's power reactor kept this room from shrinking to its true size— and crushing everything inside of it.

I jumped through the portal with a second to spare.

In retrospect, I probably should've headed someplace other than the White House lawn, especially in a stolen Nazi uniform. I was arrested on the spot and roughed up along the way. Worse, my meds wore off while I was in detention. I got so violent that they had to stick me in a padded cell. But then my FBI contacts came along and stuffed the right pills down my throat.

Anyway, I was debriefed and the feds gratefully cut me that check. All in all, everything turned out better than it should have.

Professor Ryan Eskar and Nora Eskar (his oh-so beautiful daughter) had safely arrived in Glasgow and were heading back to the U.S. Eskar was the world's leading expert on rocket guidance systems. Vindischein needed that expertise. While the mad genius could've whipped up one on his own in about three months, Hitler had moved up the invasion plans by six weeks and forced Vindischein's hand.

When the Eskars were kidnapped, on U.S. soil, the FBI got concerned and hired me to track them down. After that, it was simply a matter of using my peculiar detective skills and mad genius know-how to save the day. To think: if the short little dictator had waited a couple more months, the greatest country in the world might've fallen like a house of cards.

Apparently, the Inflato-Me had decided not to crash the IBR into the ocean. Rather, it chose to override the weapon's programming and fly the darned thing home! He pulled off a water landing near Pearl Harbor and turned it over to the military. As a result, America had obtained the world's first semi-functional nuclear weapon in the spring of 1939.

The only problem was that they had no idea how it worked. They figured it might take five years or so to reverse-engineer a suitable, low-yield, prototype. While they offered me a king's ransom to help speed things up, I politely declined for a number of reasons.

For one, being locked up with such weaponry might tip me over the edge of sanity.

Two, I needed to hire a sidekick—preferably someone lucky.

Then there was Nora, who mentioned something about wanting to "thank" me properly, over a bottle of champagne and a large bed.

Lastly, there was more evil afoot.

AN OUNCE OF PREVENTION

Victor Ross drove through light snowfall and stopped at the gated entrance of the Hule estate. The thin, tanned Brit was in his early 40's with a few traces of gray hair mixed in with the brown. Gate-mounted cameras swiveled in his direction and sized up his aging black Volvo station wagon. On the driver's side was a ten-digit keypad.

Ross reached out, entered a nine-digit security code, and patiently waited. A few seconds later, the metal gates quietly swung open. He slowly rolled up the paved drive and veered off toward the seven-car garage.

One of the estate's two dozen security guards was waiting for him. The guard wore a black suit, matching turtleneck, and wore a gray plastic earpiece in his left ear. Victor waved as he struggled to remember the young fellow's name. Dark-haired, built like a power lifter, and as polite as a brick wall, the guard gestured for him to step out of the car.

"Good morning," Victor said.

The guard grunted once in reply as he gestured for Victor to lift his arms. Victor sighed and raised his arms outward. The guard thoroughly frisked him, which was the protocol for anyone entering the grounds—even the staff.

He wasn't sure why.

The Hule family, while eccentric, wasn't in any known danger. As Ross recalled, the paranoia began soon after their daughter, Mira, was born. Being the butler, Victor felt it wasn't his place to ever ask why. None of the staff were stupid enough to risk their well-paying jobs either. The guard signaled Victor to put his arms down and headed for the back of the car.

"How was the trip?" the guard asked.

"Spectacular," Victor replied, surprised that the guard had actually spoken to him. *The brute must be having a nice day*, Victor thought as he handed his keys to the guard. "Las Vegas is a wonderful place to be this time of year."

The guard unlocked the back of the station wagon and went through Victor's luggage. This was also standard security procedure.

"I'd imagine," the guard replied with a knowing smile. "So, how much did you lose?"

"I never gamble," Victor replied.

The guard acknowledged the lie without comment. As he opened a travel bag, he spotted a bronze crucifix on a black metal chain. The guard's eyes widened as he jumped away from it.

"What is it?" Victor asked.

"The cross. Is it yours?!"

"No," Victor truthfully replied. "I never saw it before. Why?"

The guard raised his right wrist to his mouth, revealing a small wrap-around radio. He nervously spoke something in a guttural tongue that Victor never heard before. Curious, the butler pulled the crucifix from his bag and examined it in the morning light. Six inches long, it had a well-crafted likeness of Christ upon it.

Aside from its obvious value, Victor noticed two odd things about the item. One, it felt strangely warm in his hands (in spite of the winter cold). Two, the chain was looped through the bottom of the cross—not the top. Anyone wearing the chain would be sporting an upside-down crucifix.

Still, it was a pretty cross—

The front gate suddenly exploded into the Hule estate. Neither man heard a booming explosion, felt a blast wave, or saw a brilliant fireball. To their eyes, it looked as if an invisible force simply flung brick and metal aside. Victor and the guard ran out of the garage, mystified by what they just witnessed.

As the dust settled, an extremely pale man walked through the shattered remnants of the front gate. He appeared to be in his mid-30's, with a strikingly handsome—yet malevolent—face. The winter breeze played with his blondish, curly hair. Dressed in a tieless white suit, shirt, and shoes, he headed straight for the mansion with a slow menace.

"Stay here!" The guard shouted to Victor as he pulled out a Glock pistol and moved to intercept the stranger.

Five more guards ran up from the mansion, wielding assorted small arms. The stranger stopped as they formed a firing line and opened up on him without so much as a word of warning. Victor flinched as they riddled him with slugs. Victor dropped the cross in shock as he realized that the stranger—whatever he was—hadn't died yet. Blood flew from his wounds and sizzled as it hit the fresh snow.

The guards emptied their guns and began to reload. Unlike Victor, they weren't surprised that the well-dressed intruder was still on his feet—or that he eyed the guards with something akin to irritation. As the stranger's wounds quickly closed, the butler slowly backed toward the dubious safety of the garage.

Just as the guards raised their guns for another barrage, the stranger waved his hands outward. All six of the guards disappeared from view. A chill ran through Victor as he wondered what happened to them. The stranger paused, closed his eyes, and watched each guard's fate with a thin smile:

Guard #1 appeared 19,000 feet over the Sahara Desert—without a parachute.

Guard #2 appeared on a train track outside of Tokyo—right in front of an oncoming bullet train. Guard #3 appeared inside of an aquarium's shark tank—just before feeding time. Guard #4 appeared in the middle of a raging four-alarm warehouse fire—with no way out. Guard #5 appeared in the Swiss Alps—right in the path of a massive avalanche. And lastly, Guard #6 (his name was Alan, by the way) appeared in a safe house within the Gaza Strip. Currently occupied by seven armed Hamas members, he almost shot his way out.

The stranger then opened his eyes and continued onward.

Fully-regenerated, he regarded Victor for a moment and gave the butler a courteous nod. Then, he headed for the mansion. The butler was too paralyzed with fear to move as he watched the stranger reach the front doors. Like the outer gate, the front entrance collapsed inward at his approach, allowing him easy access. Once he stepped inside, things were quiet. Then gunfire, screams, and explosions echoed through the chilly air.

Victor stood rooted to the spot. Several minutes later, there was only silence again. Then Victor saw smoke rising from the upper levels of the mansion, followed soon after by flames. He saw Alice (the nanny) and Vladimir (the chef) break out through a first-story window. They ran screaming for what was left of the front gate.

The stranger exited the mansion soon after, with little Mira gently cradled in his right arm. Wrapped in a pink blanket, the infant shrieked and helplessly flailed her arms. The inhuman stranger looked tired and bruised as he slowly made his way toward the garage. Still too scared to move, Victor could only stand there and watch.

The kidnapper walked up, regarded Victor for a moment, and then picked up the crucifix. Only then did Victor look down and notice that the cross had melted the snow around it. The stranger slipped the crucifix into a pocket. With a parting nod to Victor, he turned to leave.

"W-Why did you do that?!" Victor blurted out, shaking from both cold and dread.

The stranger stopped and regarded the crying infant in his arm. Then, he turned to face Victor.

"A few of my Lord's followers were . . . overzealous," the stranger replied with a slow, ominous voice. "As a result, poor little Mira was born early. Far too early. They hid her so well that I was sent to rectify matters. And thanks, in part to you, order has been restored."

"This was about some child's birthday?" Victor asked with a confused frown. "When was Mira supposed to be born?"

The stranger hesitated for a moment and then gave Victor an icy smile.

"A few decades before the oceans turn to blood, the dead arise, and your world ends."

With that, the stranger and Mira faded from view.

THE MATH PROBLEM

Professor Gordon Mells sipped a hot cup of raspberry tea in his living room. To his right was a modest bay window, which offered him a splendid view of the full-blown winter storm outside. In his mid-50's, the thin mathematician lay on his brown leather sofa with a pair of reading glasses perched on his roundish nose. In his lap was a half-read mystery novel. His thinning gray hair had grown back after the last bout of chemotherapy. Apparently, he hadn't quit smoking soon enough. While Mells' physician had assured him that he was still in remission (his second), the professor had the nagging suspicion that the cancer would return someday. Still, with some luck, he hoped to return to Harvard in time for spring semester.

The doorbell rang.

With a frown, Mells looked out of his window and saw a stranger at his door. Tall and thin, the fellow wore a thick black overcoat and matching fedora, which kept his face in shadow. Something about this guest made Mells feel uneasy.

But the howling wind quickly reminded him that this was an awful night to be out. Even if the stranger was a door-to-door salesman, Mells might offer him a hot cup of tea before throwing him back outside. With a sigh, Mells picked up his green robe from the floor, made his way to the door, and opened it a crack.

"Professor Mells?" the stranger asked, looking down at the mathematician with a sickly pallor on his pained, elderly face. Mells guessed him to be in his mid-70's, with thinning white hair and a few days' worth of matching chin stubble. There was a thick accent to his words that Mells couldn't quite place.

"Yes?" Mells replied.

The stranger put a gloved fist over his own mouth as a brief fit of coughing seized him. Thoroughly familiar with the rigors of illness, Mells could easily empathize.

"Please, come in."

"Thank you," the stranger replied as he entered. "That's quite a storm outside, isn't it?"

"December can be quite brutal in Massachusetts," Mells replied as he closed the door and locked it. "Care for some tea?"

"I'm afraid there isn't much time for tea, Professor Mells," the stranger sighed as he started to unbutton his overcoat.

There was a certain gravity to the stranger's voice that disturbed the professor.

"I'm sorry but um . . . have we met?"

Instead of replying, the stranger faced Mells and opened his overcoat to expose a bare, wrinkled torso. Under the coat, the old man only wore black boots and a pair of faded blue jeans. For a moment, the mathematician wondered why someone would go out into sub-zero wind chill without a sweater or shirt. Then, the stranger turned around and took off his overcoat.

Mells' jaw dropped.

Some sort of golden harness was clamped onto the stranger's back. Roughly the width of his pointy shoulders, the ovular harness gave him a vaguely turtle-like appearance. It punctured his flesh, via eight large spikes: two at the base of his neck, two under his armpits, and two on each of his sides, near the kidney area. The skin around the spikes looked unblemished. Mells couldn't see a drop of blood on either the stranger or his clothes, which shouldn't be impossible.

Mells took a closer look at the shell itself. The outer edges were covered with weird glyphic symbols . .

. but at the center of it was an incredibly-complex mathematical equation. While he could make out its numbers and symbols, they moved and changed before his eyes. In essence, the equation was altering itself every few seconds.

"My God! What is that?!"

"A very heavy bomb," the stranger wearily replied as he headed for the kitchen. Mells reluctantly followed him. The elderly guest pulled out a kitchen chair and sat sideways on it.

"Did you say a bomb?" Mells asked.

"That I did, Professor Mells," the stranger patiently replied. "A most unique and destructive one. If the equation isn't solved in time, it will detonate. Attempt to remove the shell and it will explode. Answer it incorrectly and it will explode."

"You should be dead already," Mells pointed out. "You've got the equivalent of eight daggers in your body!"

"And yet I'm not," replied the stranger with grim determination. "Not yet, anyway."

"What are you?" Mells asked, mystified.

"Save my life—and those of everyone else within 20 city blocks—and I'll happily tell you."

"You want me to solve this equation, then?" Mells asked as he moved behind the stranger.

"Yes. You're the last functioning math prodigy I could find. All of the others were too afraid to try the equation."

Normally, Mells would've turned him down too. Facing death for so long had fortified his sense of self-preservation. Yet, it also made him empathize with this poor old man. Also, this threat could be thwarted by high-order mathematics. If Mells didn't save him, who could?

"How much time do we have?" Mells asked, hoping there'd be enough time for them to go somewhere remote—in case he failed.

The stranger eyed a digital clock on Mells' stove, did some math of his own, and then stroked his stubbly chin.

"Seventy-three minutes."

So much for that idea, Mells frowned to himself.

"Stay here. I'll need some paper and a pen."

The stranger nodded as Mells headed upstairs. Then he eyed the tea pot. With a painful sigh, he stood up and poured himself a cup.

Sixty-nine minutes later, the stranger sat in a Thinker pose, elbow in his lap and fist against his chin. Papers were scattered about the kitchen floor as Mells furiously scribbled and allowed his natural affinity with mathematics to flow. Normally, he could look at a problem and the answer would just jump out at him in a matter of seconds. Tonight, his natural talent had met its match in the form of an ever-shifting equation. If death weren't on the line, he'd be enjoying this challenge.

A few minutes into the effort, Mells decided to stop trying to solve the equation as it was. The equation shifts occurred at random intervals, which was just damned maddening. One part of it might change—or several. Still, if the direction of the shifts could be anticipated, he might disarm the equation in time. Mells tuned out his fear and did the cold hard math . . .

"Gotcha!" Mells shouted.

The startled stranger jumped a bit in his seat as Mells jammed his black felt-tip pen against the golden harness and started to write out his answer to the equation. Eerie moments passed as the mathematician's

pen danced against the surface of the golden harness.
Then Mells abruptly stopped in mid-scribble.

"Hit a dead-end?" The stranger asked, his face
creased with worry as he looked at the clock. They only
had three minutes left.

"No," Mells grinned. "I'm waiting for the equation
to catch up with me."

As the equation shifted into place, Mells quickly
looked it over and then triumphantly laughed as he
completed the answer. The instant he did, the equation,
the glyphs, and his answer all faded away. The spikes
on the harness disappeared too, which allowed the
golden device to fall to his kitchen floor with a loud
clatter. The bomb now looked more like a harmless
piece of gold. The stranger smiled broadly as he rose to
his feet, arched his back, and turned to face Mells.

"Thank you, Professor," he sighed. "That feels
much better."

The stranger suddenly sprouted a short salt-and-
pepper beard and became more muscular before Mells'
very eyes. His aged face shifted into that of a regally
handsome male in his early 50's. His drab attire was
suddenly replaced by a black Armani three-piece suit
with an open collar and a wine red shirt. Mells stumbled
back toward the hallway, ready to run for the door if he
had to. The stranger turned to the human and gave him
an assuring grin.

"Relax, Professor. You need not fear my wrath."

"Who are you?!"

"In days past, I was known as Zeus."

"As in the King of the Greek Gods?"

Zeus nodded.

"My sister/wife, Hera, led a rebellion against me,
took my throne and banished me to Earth in that frail
mortal form. She told me that since I loved the mortal
women so much, I could live amongst them for a year. I

was stuck inside the body of a homeless vagrant with that ticking time bomb on my back."

Zeus walked over and laid his right hand on Mells' left shoulder.

"You have saved my life, Professor. I think I should return the favor."

"What do you mean?"

"Your cancer," Zeus said as he looked down at the mathematician's chest. "It would've returned with a vengeance in another eight months. As of now, consider it gone."

"Gone?" Mells asked with a surprised smile as he suddenly felt much better.

"Gone," the god confidently replied. "Smoke your brains out and take comfort in the fact that it will never bother you again."

"Thank you."

Zeus acknowledged Mells' gratitude with a nod. Then he eyed the golden shell on the floor.

"You're more than welcome to keep—or hock—that damned thing. It's worth a fortune in today's market."

Zeus started for the door.

"Now that you're 100%, what will you do?" Mells asked.

"I was thinking about going back and retaking my throne," Zeus replied with a shrug. "But Earth can be quite a fun place when you're a full-fledged god. Hera can deal with the headaches of my realm. I think I'll stay on your world for a time."

"And do what?"

"Debauchery springs to mind," Zeus replied with a whimsical smile. "It never gets boring when you're married."

BEERGUT MALLOY

My cousin Tony was living proof that Fate's a funny bitch.

A boxing trainer for over fifteen years, he never missed a fight. When his first ex-wife was in labor with twins, Tony was in Pummelin' Ray Gibbs' corner. When his dad was being buried in Philly, Tony was in New Orleans yelling at Mighty Vin Rooks to keep his guard up. I figured that nothing short of Revelations could keep the old man from a scheduled match. What finally put him down was a ruptured appendix.

Tony called me from the ambulance. He begged me to drop whatever I was doing, hop a plane to Vegas, and back his fighter—Louis "Beergut" Malloy. The guy was something of a boxing legend and way the hell past his prime. I still promised to help out. Tony gruffly thanked me and made me swear to call him after the fight.

I stepped in because Tony was family and I owed him. He taught me everything I knew about boxing. I'd also meet Beergut Malloy. The main reason for doing this favor was that this was a big-time fight. Having been in the biz for only three years, I've never been this close to the Pay-Per-View big leagues. Impressing the Vegas fight scene could reap benefits down the road.

Right now, Joey "Redhammer" Conroy was my only fighter. At twenty-two, he was an up-and-coming middleweight with a mean left hook. His record was 15-2-1. Joey wanted to become a champ himself someday—a dream that wasn't out of his reach. When I told Joey about Cousin Tony's predicament, he asked to tag along.

So we hopped a flight to Vegas.

Joey had never seen Beergut fight before but I had. It was a common assumption that Beergut earned his moniker because of his gut. Even though he was forty pounds overweight, the fighter kept up with his training regimen and dieted like a fiend. The weight just never went away.

That was part of the irony. The other part was that Beergut was a serious non-drinker. He avoided the typical vices that fighters had to deal with—especially booze. No one ever knew him to take a drink. They said he was afraid of ending up a fuck-up of a drunk like his old man, who ran his car into a ravine and died in the resulting fireball.

Still, Beergut was an amazing fighter—a few decades ago. He was 30-and-8, with 20 wins by knockout. He retired after taking 8 straight losses. Joey wasn't surprised. That kind of losing streak would be hard for any fighter to get over. I told him different.

Beergut earned his title shot through hard work, talent, and the need to win. Back then, his younger brother was sick with some kind of bone cancer. Beergut went pro to take up his brother's medical bills. Things were great, at first. Those 30 wins he had were in a row.

I explained to Joey that Beergut wasn't that quick or that powerful. He just wouldn't fall down. In the end, he'd win fights just by trading punches for nine or ten rounds. Then, on the night of the 31st match, his brother died in the hospital. From then on, Beergut simply lost the will to fight and went through the motions.

That was sixteen years ago.

Now, Beergut had to be forty-five years old and way out of shape. Tony took him in out of pity, figuring that Beergut had something to prove. While Beergut didn't explain exactly why he came back, he stubbornly got himself reinstated and relicensed. He ignored the reporters who called him a "relic," trained relentlessly for months, and then beat the living shit out of six younger opponents in a row—all by knockout. He was being compared to Rocky in the sixth movie. Fans and bookies alike started taking him seriously. Then, Beergut demanded a title shot at the number one contender, Carlos Trivera. Trivera accepted the match because everyone knew he'd win it. He was 40-and-1, with 34 wins by knockout. He was also twenty-one years younger than Beergut. I've seen Trivera fight and watched some damned-good contenders drop at his feet in under a round. I figured I could do right by Tony just to help Beergut lose the match without losing face. Anything more than that would've been a miracle.

Joey and I made it to the arena and signed in. We found Beergut in his locker room with a mostly-empty, half-gallon bottle of Jack Daniels in his hand—less than three hours before the fuckin' fight!

Oddly enough, he wasn't so fat any more. In fact, his abs were rock-hard, his arms solid, and his chest looked pretty good. While he had some love handles and a poorly-aged face, Beergut looked like he had some mileage left in him. Too bad he was stone-drunk and passed-out. It took a few minutes of me slapping him around before he came to.

Then he peed on me, finished the bottle, and passed out again.

Some of Tony's guys showed up and gave me the score. Apparently, Mitch, Beergut's only son, had racked up a gambling debt with Louis Krylt—one of the local Vegas mob bosses. Beergut's kid owed about two hundred and fifty grand. Beergut didn't have that much money on hand, even after his six recent wins. But when Krylt learned that this idiot welcher was the son of *the* Beergut Malloy, Mr. Krylt did some math. The bookies had Beergut at four-to-one odds to win (the odds probably would've been twenty-to-one a year ago). Still, if Beergut managed to take Trivera down, Krylt could win a lot of money. Krylt had seen Beergut fight and knew what he'd endure to help a relative in need. As a result, he put two million bucks on the fight and gave Beergut a very simple choice: win the bout or wait for the police to find his kid's remains. Tony surely knew this and didn't tell me because in that scenario I wouldn't touch Beergut with a ten-foot pole.

Made me wonder if Tony was even sick. Krylt had scary connections and a very long reach. The man could end my dreams and/or my life with a phone call. So much for trying to shine. It would be a lot smarter for me to blend in, do this thing, and blow town on an early flight.

It took us another hour to wake him up. This time, Beergut made it to the bathroom, pissed in the toilet (more or less), and hopped in the shower. By the time he dried off and got dressed, the fighter had sobered up enough for a sitdown. Introductions were made and Tony's guys scurried around, getting things in order.

We talked strategy. Beergut agreed that he needed to avoid a straight-up slugfest for the first two rounds. However good he used to be, there was no way this drunk fucker could last one fuckin' round against Trivera. I told Beergut to find his shots, play defense, and to unload on Trivera in the third round. If the guy had a weakness, I'd spot it and point it own between rounds.

Looking hungover, Beergut agreed with the game plan and sincerely thanked me for helping out. With twenty minutes left before we went out, Beergut's son showed up with a brown paper bag. Inside were two fresh half-gallon bottles of Jack Daniels! I did my best impersonation of Tony in a rage, yelling that he was about to take on a champion-level contender. Beergut ignored me, opened one bottle, and drank it down like he was a living drain.

Mitch explained that Beergut knew what he was doing. Joey and I watched him drop the whole bottle in under ten seconds, pull the other one out and guzzle it dry just as fast. We couldn't believe our eyes. He should be dead from alcohol poisoning by now. No human being could down three big bottles of Jack, in one hour, and not die.

At that point, I went through the motions and got him ready. Beergut's not my fighter. It's not my kid's life at stake. All I had to do was to give Beergut advice and try to make sure that he made it to the hospital alive after he lost.

Yet, after a really long third piss, Beergut seemed to perk up. Not only did he look completely awake, he looked kinda scary—like a Viking berserker eager to go out and kill somebody.

The clock ticked.

Beergut got meaner and meaner with each passing second. He was pacing the room. Even Joey—who feared no one—stayed out of his way. When a guy came in and announced ten minutes to match time, Beergut gave me a wide, evil grin. Then he chewed up a whole pack of breath mints and led the way, humming an old Irish-sounding tune all the way to the ring. Trivera and his folks waited in the opposite corner. The huge, ugly Mexican wore a cocky smile.

I reminded him of our strategy. He nodded as I put the mouthpiece in. The announcer and the ref stood at the center. Both fighters stepped up to him, heard the rules, and slapped gloves. The bell rang. Then Beergut ran the fuck across the ring and smashed Trivera across the jaw with a hard right cross!

So much for strategy.

The entire arena went dead silent as Trivera hit the mat, half-dazed. The ref shoved Beergut back as the assembled crowd cheered. Trivera got up by the time the ref counted to six. Blood came out of Trivera's mouth and his eyes filled with humiliated rage. Joey and I swapped "oh-shit" glances. We had both seen that look in prior fights, right before Trivera exploded on some poor bastard.

Beergut was a dead man.

The ref resumed the fight.

Both men charged toward each other and started swinging as if they were being paid by the punch. Finesse and discipline went out the window. Anyone watching the match knew that this fight would be over in another round or two, tops. Trivera focused his punches on Beergut's face, clearly intending to knock his IQ down to the pre-school level. While Beergut took some nasty shots, he shrugged them off.

Even if he was too hammered to feel Trivera's hits, Beergut should've been stumbling around the ring like any other self-respecting drunk. Apparently, three bottles of Jack had the opposite effect. He moved like a man half his age as he dodged Trivera's best punches and laid into the younger boxer with some powerful body shots. They equally pounded away at each other— at first. But then one of Beergut's uppercuts caught Trivera along the left side of his ribs. The blow lifted the champ a few inches off the mat and popped the wind out of him.

Son of a bitch!

Without a hint of mercy, Beergut changed up and worked both sides of Trivera's skull with some very basic fist work. Trivera's defiant counterpunches either didn't land at all or lacked any visible effect when they did. Beergut then smashed Trivera with a left uppercut to the chin.

This time, Trivera went down and didn't move for the ten-count. Beergut roared with triumph as the ref held his arm up and declared him the winner.

Paramedics and Trivera's people rushed in to check on the poor, mangled ex-champion . . . and I kicked myself for betting my last two hundred bucks against Beergut when he was all passed out.

TWELVE SLICES

I laid the last of the offerings on my stone altar. Set in a sub-basement below my shop, it was smuggled in from a lost Mayan temple. Once used for human sacrifices, the ancient stone was still rich with power just waiting to be used for something new. I added non-Mayan glyphs and sigils to the stone with an artist's care. The enchantments I laid down were the mystical equivalent of program code, setting firm parameters with fail safes meant to keep the different magicks from rejecting each other. The altar itself was surrounded by shelves, each packed with the tools of my trade. The problem with not being a pure-blooded mystic was that I needed more props to get anything done. A mage was born with it. True witch types sold their souls for it. Dabbler-occultists, like myself, had to rely on exotic gear, skill, and months of preparation.

Tonight, I was going to reach into the not-so-deepest pits of Hell and extract the troubled soul of one Vic Daparza. He flipped pizzas for me during high school, joined the Army for a while, and then got sucked into the merc trade. Someone convinced him that the private sector was a better way to pay the bills.

In simpler times, that might've been the case. Then poor Vic got himself killed in some shit-stained place I can't even pronounce. They brought him home last month for a closed-casket ceremony. I was friends with his family so I used that as a way into the wake. During visiting hours, I snuck in with my compass. Unlike its standard field counterpart, this one either pointed north or south.

North was Heaven. South wasn't.

As I looked over at Vic's grieving widow and infant son, I figured he'd be a good candidate. Of course, one never knew when it came to recruiting the damned. On top of that, I had to hurry. Contrary to Christian teachings, souls didn't spend an eternity in Hell. They got hunted down and eaten. Hell was something of a safari for demons, who consumed the damned until they gained enough power to break free. I've even heard of souls eating other souls, hoping to evolve into demons themselves—not just to get off the menu but to escape. Every time one of the horned fucks crossed over, the barriers between the mortal world and Hell weakened. When the last barrier falls . . .

In older times, demons were vigorously hunted down and slaughtered. Now, they've gotten wiser and way more discreet. Able to mingle with humanity, they've used magic to conceal their plots. If the rumors were true, a few of 'em even made it into the White House.

These days, thanks to our ever-expanding population of Hell-bound sinners, Judgment Day's in the near future. I can't stop it but I can do my civic duty. Assuming Vic's soul hadn't been consumed, I'd send him out into a world of disbelief. Where the few of us who knew how magic worked typically used it for selfish ends. Instead of "hexting" my ex-wife or turning plastic into gold, I figured on using my skills to do something truly stupid.

"All right," I said to myself. "Let's do this."

I laid the extra-large, twelve-slice pizza on the center of the altar. Fresh out of the oven, it was buried with fresh toppings. I then poured powders and potions around it. Then I invoked Them. Twelve slices of pizza for twelve Spirits of Light.

Months were spent negotiating terms. In ancient times, they were known to be aloof and unwilling to help mortals. Now, they were lonely. Forgotten for so long, they were thrilled to have anyone ask them for anything. Fuckers were so desperate that they each lent me their powers for a slice of pizza.

Still, I showed them respect.

So now, kneeling on aching knees, I prayed for their power. Their voices joined mine as I closed my eyes and chanted the invocation. Suddenly, there was a crackling of magicks and a wave of energy rippled from the altar. If not for my fail safes, the energy might've leveled a city block (or five). Trembling with hope, I opened my eyes and examined my handiwork.

Unconscious and covered with cuts lay the solid soul of Vic Daparza. In his mid-30's, the poor guy was still in his military-style fatigues. Strong-chinned and handsome, his tanned face was locked in the throes of pain. I wanted to wake Vic up and ask how he ended up in Hell. That wasn't going to happen because the less Vic knew about me, the safer I was.

Once I sent him into the field, others would want to know where he came from. I'd be at risk, as would those close to me. Then there was Vic himself. This muscular soul wasn't the skinny kid I met so many years ago. He might kill me instead of thank me, especially once the spirits told him the price of his resurrection.

Basically, he was to become a mystical hitman. They'd point Vic at targets and he'd kill them with the powers they had just given him. Evil occultists and rogue demons would be his primary targets. Saving innocents was a secondary priority because of the stakes.

Best of all, these powers could be bestowed to others.

Much like a blessing, Vic could grant any worthy mortal both his powers and mission. The spirits would

guide them and (just maybe) they could slow down our
all-but-certain doom. As much as I'd like to hope, I
knew better. Demons were walking the earth and the
barrier between planes weakened by the day.
This wouldn't be enough.
But that's the thing about God. He/she/whatever
had a plan. I'd lived enough centuries to know that
much. Hopefully, Vic ended up more of the solution
than the problem.
With a sigh, I put on some gloves and then grabbed
a black suitcase. Inside were clothes, walk-around
money, four loaded handguns, and three fake IDs. I
slapped the suitcase onto Vic's soul. Awkwardly
balanced, the altar held it (and Vic) in place like they
were glued together. I then slapped my hands together
and they disappeared.
Destination: a rooftop several miles from here. Vic
awakened there and the spirits took it from there . . .

A WORK OF ART

Gabe Diermond stood on a fog-shrouded edge of the Brooklyn Bridge ready to jump to his death. The flabby Caucasian had thinning brown hair, a thick mustache, and an utterly despondent look on his face. In his mid-40's, he wore a rumpled gray suit and reeked of alcohol following a four-hour drinking binge.

As he eyed the darkened waters below, Gabe removed his striped necktie, gold watch, and black leather wallet. He gently placed them all on the walkway as he fought back tears. Then he eyed his gold wedding band, which rarely left his finger during seven years of devoted marriage. With effort, he pulled it off his finger and tossed it over the side.

His wife, Elaine, was the cause of his suicidal urge.

Supposedly pregnant with their first child, she had just left him to marry Wes Loch—his boss. Rather than tell him to his face, she simply packed up a few of her belongings and taped a note to the front door of their apartment. Elaine's letter simply declared that she wanted a divorce and that she had been screwing Wes for about a year. It offered no apology for the affair, which went on while her loyal, loving husband was working long hours to earn a promotion to buy a house. Gabe might've endured this had she not ended the letter by stating that the baby girl wasn't his.

That callous revelation put a hole right through him.

While some New Yorkers probably would've hunted them both down with large-caliber weapons, Gabe was too deeply in love to ever hurt her. Thus, he opted to get stumbling drunk and then end his misery with a quick leap off a high bridge. Gabe was eager to jump, hoping to find some peace in death.

Suddenly, Beshem stepped out of the nearby fog with two beefy, well-dressed men on either side of him. In his late 30's, the hawk-faced mute wore a burgundy suit on a wiry frame, with a black ponytail that snaked below his shoulder blades. As Gabe closed his eyes and braced himself for that one last dive, Beshem gave his men the nod.

The two underlings surged forward like twin bulls after a red-caped matador. Gabe never noticed them until they grabbed him . . . right as he jumped. Their combined strength yanked him back with ease.

"Hey!" Gabe struggled in vain, as his feet clumsily hit the walkway. "What the hell are you doing?!"

The two brutes said nothing as they forced Gabe onto his back. Gabe struggled and cursed as Beshem walked up with a white handkerchief and a bottle of chloroform. He administered a reasonable dosage into the cloth and then slapped it firmly over Gabe's mouth. The trio waited until he blacked out.

Gabe groggily woke up on a black leather couch in the living room of a huge, airy loft. Half-blinded by the bright morning sun, he squinted at the cream-colored walls, high-vaulted ceiling, and opulent furnishings. In a panic, he jumped to his feet, which ignited a vicious hangover. For a moment, Gabe had to steady himself. Then he walked over to the penthouse's wall-sized windows and easily recognized the not-so-distant Manhattan skyline.

"I hope you're not planning to try another jump," a deep, lightly-accented voice teased. "The other tenants might hold it against me."

Gabe turned to see a handsome black man standing behind him. Tall, confident, and built like a ripped runway model, he walked over with a perfect grin on his face. He wore a tieless black suit, white shirt, and looked to be in his late thirties. What stood out the most to Gabe were the man's grayish eyes. Somehow, they looked much older.

"Who are you?" Gabe asked with an angry edge.

"Call me 'C'—as in 'Cupid,'" replied his host. "Sorry if my people roughed you up."

"Whatever this is about, C, I think you snatched the wrong guy."

"My business is with you, Gabe," C replied as he headed for the kitchen. "But don't worry. This is a good thing."

Gabe scoffed at that last part.

"You hungry?" C asked. "I've got some steaks in the fridge."

Gabe's stomach audibly rumbled. His face slightly reddened as he followed C into a decked-out kitchen. C reached into an enormous fridge and pulled out two bottles of water. He tossed one to Gabe and set his own on a marble counter.

"Excuse me," Gabe frowned as he set the bottle down and gently rubbed his aching brow. "But, um, how is kidnapping me a good thing?"

"For starters, you're not an oversized pool toy right now," C mused as he opened the freezer and pulled out a two-pack of gourmet steaks.

Gabe felt a pang of misery run through him as he remembered why he tried to end his life. He wasn't relieved that he was still alive—not one bit. Gabe opened his water, hoping it was poisoned. But something told him that his kidnapper/host didn't mean him any harm.

"And living's a better thing?" Gabe asked.

"Depends on the situation and how it's viewed," C replied. "You're about to lose your two-timing wife, without having to pay child support or squabble over marital assets. And right now, you could probably blackmail your boss for that elusive annual bonus. Most 40-somethings in your shoes would be touring titty bars to celebrate."

"Guess I fall outside of your demographic," Gabe muttered as he took a sip.

"No, Gabe, you're smack-dab in the middle of it. You're madly in love. Not the 'lip-service' kind that results in endless fights and eventual divorce. It's genuine love: the kind where the pain of betrayal never quite goes away."

Gabe flinched as Beshem entered the kitchen in the same clothes he had on the night before. The creepy fellow handed C a folded letter and a plate-sized mirror. Then he turned and nodded to Gabe with a polite smile. C set the mirror on the countertop and unfolded the letter.

"Gabe, this is Beshem," C muttered as he skimmed the letter's contents. "He can't talk. But he's one of the best people I've ever made."

Beshem held out his hand.

Gabe reluctantly shook it and was about to thank the mute for saving his life . . . then paused. C didn't say "I've ever met." He said, "I've ever made."

C finished the letter and handed it to Beshem.

"That's a pretty tall order," C grinned as he opened a nearby cabinet and reached in for some plates. "You sure his heart can handle it?"

Beshem offered an innocent shrug in reply.

"Ah well," C said, as he set down the plates. "With the money he pays me, I guess I shouldn't object. Still, the Sheik's pushing eighty."

C snapped his fingers and a light-skinned Asian beauty appeared out of thin air! Gabe jumped back a step and then took her in. Smelling of lilacs, she wore a

dark-blue mini-skirt over her lithe, well-endowed frame.
Her long, black hair came down to the small of her back.
The black stiletto heels, in Gabe's opinion, were a nice
touch. Her beauty made even the sad man's heart skip a
beat.

"What do you think, Gabe? Too tall?" C asked as
he pulled off some strips of paper towel from a roll on
the wall.

"How'd you do that?!"

"Family secret," C grinned as he gestured for his
creation to follow Beshem. She made a kissing gesture
in Gabe's direction as Beshem led her out of the kitchen.
C headed for the fridge and opened the freezer.

"You just *made* a woman!"

"Cool, huh?" C replied as he unwrapped the steaks
and put them on the plates. "Not only is she an 11 on
the scale of 1-to-10, but she's got skills to boot."

"What do you mean?" Gabe asked.

"I make people to the specs of the buyer," C
explained. "You want a super genius who looks like a
super model? Pay me. Nymphomaniac twins who'll
never be tired of your boring personality? Pay me.
Some of the most talented sex symbols in the world
today were made by yours truly."

C dropped both steaks on the plates, waved his left
hand over them, and the frozen meat was suddenly
cooked.

"Hope you like yours medium-well."

Gabe gawked as C walked over to a drawer and
pulled out a pair of knives and forks.

"Why am I here?" Gabe asked, clearly mystified.

C's mood fell a bit as he handed Gabe a knife and
fork.

"You want some A-1? A baked potato, maybe?"

Gabe snatched his silverware and rudely threw
them aside.

"No! I want to know what I'm doing here!"
C sighed as he set his own silverware down and
picked up his bottled water. The pimp paced a bit as he
unscrewed the cap and sought the right words.
"My business is to make people happy," C
explained. "I've been at it for a very long time. And,
like in all businesses, the occasional problems arise. In
this case: you."
"Me?"
"Yes. See, you're one of mine."
Gabe was speechless.
"Your father-in-law paid me a ton of money to
make someone capable of being a good husband and
provider for his baby girl, who was growing up to be
quite the cold-hearted bitch."
"That can't be right!" Gabe countered. "You
'make' beautiful people for sheiks and other rich people
who can afford it! Why would he pay you good money
to make me as I am?! Why not make 'Prince Charming'
or something?"
"As I recall, he wanted to," C grinned. "But Frank
could only afford an average guy . . . you. And looks
aside, the love you two felt was very real. I crafted it
myself."
Gabe paused to think back.
His father-in-law, Frank, owned a small chain of
struggling furniture stores. Gabe remembered that Frank
had just started having financial difficulty soon after the
wedding. At present, the furniture chain was a hair's
breath away from bankruptcy. Frank's wife had died
years ago and he didn't have any other children. Had his
father-in-law really jeopardized his family business just
to make sure his daughter would end up happy?
"He wanted a good man with a big heart and a love
for sports," C continued. "Someone who'd work extra
hard to make her happy–"

"I'm not some pimp's goddamned conjuration!"
Gabe yelled. "I was born and raised in Philly!"
"Fake memories," C replied.
"And my parents, brothers, and sister—"
"I made them," Gabe patiently interrupted. "Part of
the package. He wanted you to have a big family, so I
also made aunts, uncles, cousins, and your four nephews.
You're all about eight years old, Gabe."
Gabe looked down at the floor and tried to digest
this bizarre revelation.
"So what happened?"
"Frank couldn't keep up with his payments," C
sadly grinned. "It happens sometimes. And when it
does, I give my clients something of a 'grace period' to
fix things. I haven't had a default in . . . many a moon."
"So, you're like the gas company or something?"
Gabe sneered. "You can just 'turn off the love' with the
flick of a switch?"
C took a sip of water and considered the question
for a moment.
"You know I've never really tried that. See, Love's
a powerful thing—even if it's manipulated. Abruptly
stopping a pair of tornados would be a lot easier than
breaking true love. But I can undo my own handiwork.
So, once Frank's grace period ended, I set things back to
the way they were. In the end, she stopped loving you.
But since you were made to love her, you couldn't stop."
Gabe chewed on that for a moment.
"Does she really love him?"
"Your boss?" C asked.
Gabe nodded.
"I'm afraid so," the matchmaker sadly replied.
"The irony's that they never would've met if it weren't
for you. In the end, they'll probably do just fine—even
with her expensive tastes."

"What about Frank? How much does he still owe
you?"
"I just hit him up for that couch you woke up on," C
grinned. "As of now, he doesn't owe me a dime. With a
bit of luck and time, his business should recover."
"So what now? Are you going to 'uncreate' me or
something?" Gabe asked.
"No," C replied with a shake of his head. "Frank
feels pretty bad about the whole thing. When he found
out about his daughter's infidelity, he called me up and
asked me to make it up to you."
Gabe rolled his eyes. "Oh really? How are you
gonna do that?"
"Pick up the mirror," C replied with a clever smile
as he stepped back and sipped his water.
"Why?!" Gabe asked, clearly exasperated.
"Just do it."
Gabe picked up the mirror with his left hand. His
reflection was now that of someone else—a handsomer,
younger man in his early 20's with curly black hair. His
rumpled suit was now black, pressed, and far more
stylish. Even his hangover was gone.
He looked down, expecting to see his older self . . .
but didn't.
"What is this?!" Gabe asked as he ran his right hand
through his new head of hair. Even his voice had
changed.
"It's the new you. All you have to do is walk out of
my front door, Gabe. Your memories will change. The
ID in your wallet will change. You'll start a new life as
an up-and-coming poet with a gift for gab and a heart of
gold. Women will be all over you."
"And what about my family?"
"They'll forget about you, as will the outside world.
It'll be as if Gabe Diermond never existed. Meanwhile,
this new 'you' is an orphan with a trust fund and a

promising life. I'll throw in a few good friends to keep you amused. But best of all, you start off with a very clean slate and no pesky heartbreak. You can even pick your new name."

"Why are you doing this? If I'm nothing more than a product, you could've just let me jump off that bridge and be done with it."

"I know," C replied. "But what kind of an artist would I be if I let my one of my masterpieces kill himself? Besides, I keep hearing that good men are hard to find."

"That's no way to run a business," Gabe mildly countered.

"I disagree," C replied with a thoughtful grin. "Top-rate customer service is one of the basic tenants of good business. For example, by sparing you and giving you a new life, Frank walks away satisfied."

"So what? He's almost broke."

"Yes, Frank's almost broke. But his high-end customers and contacts aren't. Seeing as my business depends upon word-of-mouth referrals, your ex-father-in-law will send new clients my way. Satisfied customers always do."

C took a swig of water. Gabe sat on a stool and set the mirror down, the idea of a fresh start growing on him.

"Thank you," came Gabe's earnest reply.

C replied with a wink and a silent toast. "Anything else?"

"Yeah. Could I have some clean silverware, paper, and a pen, please?" Gabe asked with a smile. "I feel a poem coming on."

THE ANTIQUE

Ilya Damerski materialized inside of his immense storage vault with a soft implosion of air. The pale time thief was a short, stocky man in his late forties, with thinning black hair and weathered features. He wore a colonel's black Gestapo uniform and carried a first edition military strategy book in both hands. Wrapped in a protective paper binding, the book was written by General Erwin Rommel, with his autograph on the inside of the front cover.

Pleased by his latest acquisition, Damerski climbed five flights of metal stairs and walked past shelves of military artifacts. Each item was stored in a stasis box, which would both artificially age the items he collected and preserve them to a point where they could still be auctioned off. The stasis boxes were the key to his entire operation. With them, he could steal coins from the era of Alexander the Great—while they were still new—and then age them thousands of years inside of a week. By the time he pulled them out, they'd look nice enough to bring in serious cash but also "old" enough to fool carbon dating technology. Naturally, he pawned his artifacts in the past—well before stasis boxes were invented.

Each stasis box was of a different size—from that of a cigar box to a large refrigerator. Their housings were made of a transparent metal, which allowed Damerski to view the contents as they aged (which always appealed to the collector in him). He placed Rommel's book in its small stasis box, between a spear used by Shaka Zulu and a gun belt once worn by Robert E. Lee.

"Status?" Damerski called out in fluent German, as he headed for the hypno-programming bay.

144 · Marcus V. Calvert

He always put himself through a hypno-programming regimen before jumping back into a particular period. While he was really from Orono, Maine (circa 2254), the hypno-programming could make him walk, talk, and think like a Gestapo colonel would. After a jump, Damerski could simply sit in the hypno-programming bay and have his computer restore him to his normal self inside of five minutes.

"Vault integrity has been breached," a male voice replied in German.

Damerski's jaw dropped. In the fifteen years he had been pilfering from the timestream, no one had ever broken into his vault. After all, it was located at the bottom of a crater on the moon—in 1841! While he had assumed that his inner sanctum would never be breached, he had the foresight to install a top-of-the-line security system with AI-controlled weaponry.

"Elaborate," Damerski ordered, as he drew his sidearm—a modified Luger pistol with an optional energy blaster setting.

"Ninety-two minutes ago, five armed intruders time-jumped into the vault, near the records lab. Intrusion countermeasures were sufficient to subdue them."

Damerski ran down five flights of stairs, enraged that someone would dare attempt to steal from him. Worse, the "Nazi" in him thought of a dozen visceral ways to make them suffer.

"How many dead?" he growled.

"Four," the computer replied. "The apparent leader was stunned and kept alive per programming parameters."

"Good," Damerski replied as he continued his descent.

Damerski carefully rounded a corner, pistol raised, and then stopped dead in his tracks at the sight before him. Five men were bound in electro nets, which were shot out of launchers hidden throughout the room. The thief cocked his head as he eyed their Colonial-era garb. His keen eye estimated that they were fashionable around the late 1700's. Four of the intruders were charred black by the electro nets, which the AI set for lethal shocks. The last one was conscious but unable to move. A flintlock-style pistol lay just beyond his reach. Damerski enabled the Luger's blaster setting and kicked the intruder's weapon away. The Gestapo hypno-programming urged him to use torture (and lots of it). Instead, the time thief gave his captive a curt nod.

"I think you're lost, my friend," Damerski said in accented English.

"You must be Ivan Damerski," the captive sighed with an exhausted smile and a Bostonian accent. "Please forgive our intrusion."

"Who are you? And what are you doing in my vault?"

"My name's Marcus Aslowe," replied the intruder. "My team and I were sent here to retrieve something you've stolen."

"And that would be?"

Aslowe hesitated. Damerski fired at the corpse of one of Aslowe' men—just past the waistline. The blast left a plate-sized hole in the floor and split the body in half.

"That's the mood I'm in," Damerski callously replied as he pointed the gun at Aslowe's right knee. "Now, why are you here?"

Aslowe nervously licked his dry lips.

"We came for a grandfather clock which belonged to Ben Franklin."

Damerski remembered stealing it two months ago, less than five weeks after Franklin's death in 1790. He hadn't gotten around to finding a buyer for it.

"What's so important about this clock?"

"He hid his AI inside of it."

"Ben Franklin's a time traveler?!" Damerski chuckled with surprise.

Aslowe gravely nodded. Damerski shrugged and crouched over his captive.

"The man was always ahead of his time," muttered the time thief. "Speaking of which, when did you come from, Mr. Aslowe?"

"2409."

Damerski was really intrigued now. His time machine was only able to go into the past and back. Aslowe might be packing technology so advanced that Damerski could go into his own future. Dozens of profitable schemes began to hatch within his keen mind.

"And this AI does what?"

"It ran a number of global spy satellites, which we had positioned in the past," Aslowe explained. "These satellites allowed us to monitor world events—so that we could alter them."

"What kind of world were you trying to shape?"

"In my time period, Earth is run by military rule. It was the only way to maintain order in the face of rampant population growth and diminishing resources. Our goal was to install our version of rule within one of the old colonial powers, while avoiding the mistakes of our ancestors."

"Let me guess—the British Empire?"

Aslowe nodded, a bit shocked by the accuracy of Damerski's guess.

"We'll make a better world: one where democracy, communism, theocracy, and tyranny won't doom us to extinction. A modified monarchy would be the best way to achieve this."

"You should've contacted your future comrades for assistance," Damerski mused, as he looked over Aslowe's dead friends. "Why didn't you?"

"Our temporal communicator was within the AI," Aslowe sighed as he eyed the ceiling. "Also, my government doesn't look kindly on failure. And this particular 'incident' would've earned both of us a bullet to the head."

Damerski grinned, conceding the point. Losing a temporal AI was an inexcusable failure.

"We had enough tech to scrape together a crude time device and track the energy signature of your time jump," Aslowe continued. "We only had to cross sixty years to get here."

"I sense that you're being honest with me," Damerski admitted.

"Good," Aslowe replied with a tight smile. "Now name your price. I'm sure we can work this out."

Damerski paused to consider the offer. "It's a tempting offer."

Aslowe smiled up with fragile hope in his eyes.

"But I don't think your plan will work."

Aslowe's eyes narrowed.

"Why not?"

"It's simple: the British aren't good enough to rule the world," Damerski said matter-of-factly. "I'd go with a different group of people altogether. You'd need people with a more 'efficient' world view."

"What? Like a German Reich of some kind?!" Aslowe scoffed, as he eyed Damerski's uniform. "Even if they were a unified nation at this point in history, they'd never be up for the task!"

"Oh? And what do you have against Germans, Mr. Aslowe?" Damerski evenly asked.

"I'm Jewish. That's reason enough."

"Ah," Damerski replied. "A pity."

Aslowe gawked as he saw the barrel of the weapon line up with his face and fire. Even with the Gestapo hypno-programming, the time thief would've killed Aslowe for the trespass.

Damerski holstered his weapon, ordered the AI to have repair bots clean up the mess, and then walked up two flights of stairs. He found the grandfather clock, opened it, and eyed its apparently-normal mechanisms.

"Are you capable of independent thought?"

"Negative," the clock's AI replied. "My creators feared a repeat of the AI insurrection of 2391. I must obey the commands of any human being born after the 21st century."

"Identify me," Damerski said with a grin, not bothering to wonder why those fools hadn't set more stringent security protocols.

The air around him shimmered with some transparent energy wave.

"Identification scans complete. Subject is Ivan Damerski. Date of birth, November 9th, 2214."

"You will obey my commands?"

"Affirmative," replied the AI.

"Good," Damerski replied. "I need you to run a few historical scenarios for me."

"Parameters?"

"Had your previous users managed to extend British rule over the planet, what was the estimated probability of the human race not facing extinction by the 25th century?"

"23.0154%," came the AI's reply.

"Reset parameters for another query."

"Ready," the AI stated.

"If the world was conquered by the 19th-century equivalent of a Third Reich, and its rule sustained until 2409, what is the probability that the human race would avoid extinction?"

"72.8276%."

The "Nazi" in him smiled.

The American in him shuddered.

Unsure of what to do, Damerski eventually settled on letting Fate decide. He powered down the AI and walked over to one of the smaller stasis boxes. Inside was the very first Kennedy half-dollar. He opened the box and pulled out the silvery coin. He admired Kennedy's likeness in his gloved hand for a moment, chose "heads," and then flipped the coin.

If the coin came up heads, then Damerski would try his hand at reaching that 72.8276% probability. With enough patience and care, he could sculpt a thousand-year Reich that could preserve the world.

If it came down tails, Damerski would use the AI to do some research on the future and then loot the hell out it (in terms of useful technology). Along the way, the time thief would see what he could do about saving mankind's future. Something told him that the solution(s) to their problems were right in front of them.

As far as Damerski was concerned, just about anything could be fixed with a little judicious time travelling. It might be as simple as a watered-down sterility plague, negating a few horrendous events, and/or killing a few historical figures in their futuristic cribs.

Only time would tell.

With a deft hand, the time thief flipped the coin into the air.

A RABBI AND A DEMON

"A rabbi and a demon walk into a bar."

Every time I think of them, those words dance in my head like the start of an old, bad joke. Yeah, it actually happened . . . only they walked into a diner instead of a bar. It was my ninth day on the job. We had a packed house thanks to a busload of tourists headed west. The night was dark and stormy outside.

About twenty minutes into the storm, they entered.

The rabbi looked the part of an Orthodox Jew—down to the brimmed black hat, matching suit, white shirt, and hanging locks. His only unusual feature was the pair of black leather gloves he wore, seeing as it was July and all. Judging from the weathered face and graying black beard, I'd say he was in his early fifties.

While the rabbi must've been about 5'8" or so, the demon was at least 6'5" and ripped as hell. Dressed like a biker, the demon looked human (at first). His leather-and-denim attire was an oddly-stylish blend of black and red. He had more than a few days of stubble and shoulder-length black hair.

I was taking orders by the door so I could hear them speak. The rabbi stroked his beard, closed his eyes, and prayed. I dated a Jewish guy once, so I knew Hebrew when I heard it. When he finished, the rabbi looked over at the demon.

"How many?" the rabbi asked.

The demon's dark brown eyes took in the crowded diner like a wolf in a henhouse. I glanced into the demon's blue eyes as they fell on me. His stare violated me. Like he had ripped every secret from me and read them all in an instant.

"Three folks in the kitchen, that family of four in the back," the demon replied, before nodding my way, "and the waitress over here."

"I hate working on the Sabbath," the rabbi frowned.

"I suppose we can take the weekend off," the demon replied with a sarcastic grin. "A few dozen child-sacrificing hellspawn stop to have snacks in a roadside diner, less than ten miles from an orphanage full of cute little kids. What's the worst that could happen?"

The rabbi turned to the demon and gave him a "stop-being-a-smartass" glare.

"You know what to do. Spare the innocent. Kill the rest."

For a moment, I wondered if these two were disgruntled lunatics with a hatred of tourists and plenty of guns. As I started to edge away from them, the demon's skin color shifted into a deep gray. A pair of black horns punched through his forehead as his hair receded into his skull. His pearly-whites turned spiked as he brushed me aside with a feral smile.

"Pardon me," the demon muttered as he grabbed my customer (an elderly woman in her 60's) by the throat. He plucked her out of the booth like she didn't weigh almost two hundred pounds (and she did). I stepped back in horror as she gasped for air.

Before I could say anything, the demon threw her across the diner with frightening ease. Her skull and neck disappeared into the brand new hole in the wall. Green ichor spurted from her crushed head as gravity dragged her earthward. There was absolutely no doubt that the old lady was dead by the time she hit the floor.

The place was silent for a moment as everyone watched the old lady bleed out. Then everyone else in the dining area (except for me and the family of four in the back), roared like enraged grizzly bears . . . and changed. They sprouted blood-red fur and grew a half-foot in size. Their clothes ripped at the sudden changes in height and musculature, as their faces went monstrous and their eyes turned dark green.

Even the corpse of the dead old lady turned!

"Pyac 'La," the rabbi muttered as he drew a pair of fancy little machine pistols from under his coat. "Why'd they have to be Pyac 'La?"

"We're just lucky that way!" the demon joyously yelled as he plowed into four more monsters.

I was scared motionless as the rabbi protectively hopped in front of me and started blasting with short bursts. Any Pyac 'La that came near us ended up with a fatal head wound.

Meanwhile, the demon stood at the center of the diner and killed any monster that came within arm's reach. Even though he fought like a street brawler, the biker demon never got hit. He blocked or dodged every blow with ease. Bodies flew everywhere and any butt-ugly beast he knocked down stayed down.

The rabbi ran out of ammo. Rather than reload, he dropped the guns, and pulled two more from under his suit jacket. Six Pyac 'La moved toward the human family of four in the back corner. The rabbi turned his guns on the monsters but didn't risk the shot. Instead, he uttered another Hebrew prayer.

The six monsters slammed into some sort of invisible barrier and fell back. The rabbi merely smiled and then gunned them down, along with three more Pyac 'La who tried to blindside him from the right. Some of his shots harmlessly ricocheted off the barrier. The innocent family safely cowered under its protection.

At this point, the fight was all but over. Only five were left and two of them tried to run. One jumped for a window, only to bounce off it like a handball. Another tried to open the swinging door to the kitchen. It wouldn't budge. For a second, I wondered how that could be. Then I remembered the rabbi's first prayer. It must've been to seal the place so that the Pyac 'La couldn't run. The clever rabbi gunned the two fleeing monsters down. The remaining three jumped the demon at once— and died trying.

The biker caught the first Pyac 'La by the throat with his left hand and punched through the second one's skull with his right. As brains and bone flew through the air, the demon lowered his head into the third—and gored her like a bull. The gored Pyac 'La gawked down at her punctured boobs, slid off his horns, and then died on the way to the floor. Her green blood ran down the demon's face as he easily lifted the last Pyac 'La off the floor, his left-handed grip still around his throat. The squirming beast growled something in his native tongue.

The horned demon grinned.

"No one says those things about my mother . . . even if they are true!"

Then the demon exhaled reddish fire into the Pyac 'La's face. As the beast writhed in burning agony, the demon held on firmly until his furry skull melted. The fires didn't seem to hurt the demon or even his biker attire. He then dropped the corpse and paced about the diner, searching for someone else to kill but there weren't any other Pyac 'La left alive. Even I could see that.

Then the demon looked our way and headed toward us with that same kill-happy grin. The rabbi looked worried for a moment and half-raised his weapons. I was about to suggest that we run like hell when the demon stopped in his tracks. The half-human winced with annoyance and held up his wrists. I could see squiggly lines tattooed around both of his wrists, which now glowed with a bluish light. They reminded me of manacles.

"I think the bonds are weakening," announced the demon with a part-elated/part-worried look on his face as he shifted back into human form. The glow abruptly ceased.

"I hope you're wrong," replied the rabbi. For a half-second, it looked as if the rabbi was about to blast his partner. Instead, he holstered his weapons and picked up his discarded ones as well.

Then the rabbi turned to me with a fatherly grin.

"How's the soup here?"

PIMP MY SPY CAR

Harriet Simms stepped away from the Hertz Rental Car booth and wheeled her small burgundy carry-on bag toward the parking lot. In her late 40's, the ebony-skinned widow was attractive, short, and sported a black shoulder-length weave. A day of connecting flights from her native Chicago had wrinkled her navy-blue pantsuit. With a sigh, she checked her watch and saw that it was 11:04 p.m., Miami time.

A layer of fatigue, sweat, and determination covered Harriet's face as she briskly walked along in her low heels. The lot was filled with hundreds of cars, well-lit, and sprawled in all directions. This late at night, she happened to be the only customer walking the lot. While this might've bothered Harriet on any other occasion, tonight she was distracted.

Tomorrow was the big day.

Harriet was about to sign papers on her first published novel. Being a successful author was her life's dream . . . until her law firm internship turned into a permanent "career" as a paralegal. Long hours, marriage, kids, bills, and so many other realities buried that dream. In time, being a good wife and mother trumped literary achievement.

Heath, her husband, died from a stroke three years ago. His passing was something of a wake-up call that life was too short to waste on regrets. A few weeks later, Harriet bought a cheap notebook computer and began to churn out short stories. In spite of her nagging self-doubts, Harriet submitted them to any magazine she could find. She received sixty-seven rejection letters in the first year alone. Instead of giving up, Harriet learned from her mistakes and sharpened her skills.

She joined writers' groups, completed online research, and kept on writing. Two years into her crusade, Harriet sold her first short story. By then, she had more than enough finished pieces to put together an anthology collection. With last year's tax refund, Harriet started her own one-woman LLC (*Ungeneric Press*) and found an online print-on-demand firm to self-publish her first book. To her relief, the whole thing—down to the bland cover—cost less than a thousand bucks.

To her surprise, they sold like crazy.

Her friends at work loved her stories, most of which were themed around family struggles and the joys and pains of modern living. Copies of her book were passed around, allowing word to spread. Somehow, her book ended up in the hands of Griefson & Ross Publishing. The small, Miami-based publisher challenged her to turn one of her short stories into a full-on novel. If she could produce a viable copy, they'd publish it. The agreement wasn't contractual but they offered the pro bono services of Ted Merges, one of their editors, to proof her work.

The driven first-timer put her finished rough draft in Merges' hands within three months. Then, like a cruel English professor, he "cut" it up with his red pen . . . and told her that it was awesome. With some polish, it was just the sort of story Griefson & Ross would happily publish. So Harriet rewrote the thing (twice) and made it as close to perfection as she could. Then she turned it in and waited four months for an answer . . .

They loved it.

Griefson & Ross asked her to fly down to Miami and discuss the terms. She didn't have an agent (nor did she need one). After 20 years as a paralegal, Harriet had seen enough contract negotiations to muddle through without a pesky middleman. She had done her homework, too. The paralegal/writer tracked down other authors who had worked with Griefson & Ross. Most of them assured her that the publishing house would be fair in their dealings. A few even showed her copies of their contracts. Harriet read through them enough to (almost) draft one from memory.

At this point, all Harriet wanted to do was drive to her hotel, crank up the air conditioner, and sleep a few hours. With a yawn, she glanced down at her rental ticket and headed toward the location of her compact car. The lady at the rental desk told her to look for a gray 2015 Ford Focus two-door.

Instead, she found an ocean-blue 2016 Ford Expedition SUV with a white interior. The four-door beast of a vehicle was covered with dozens of little scratches along its hood, windshield, and driver's side door. She wondered if someone drove it through a rose garden or something.

"They gave me the wrong damned car," Harriet muttered to herself.

The tired author sized up the Expedition and decided to go back to the rental booth and yell at someone—

When a silenced bullet whizzed past her left ear and left a fresh little scratch on the Expedition's hood—just like the hundreds of other tiny scratches. Harriet ducked low with a scream. Luggage and purse forgotten, she hit the UNLOCK button on the key chain's remote. To her relief, Harriet heard a soft *click* from inside the Expedition, opened the driver's side door, and scrambled inside. As soon as she slammed it shut, Harriet hit the door locks and fumbled for the key.

Under the SUV's interior lighting, she barely noticed that the silvery key was jagged on both sides with a thin piece of plastic in the middle, much like a reshaped micro-chip. Harriet jammed the key into the ignition and gave it a twist. Her fiendishly-clever plan was to drive away really fast and not get shot along the way. Instead, nothing happened. The engine didn't even try to turn over.

Her hands shaking, Harriet spent the next few seconds wondering what the hell to do next. She ducked low to make herself less of target, and then pulled her green cell phone out of her left pocket. As she was about to dial 9-1-1, Harriet noticed someone running up to the right side.

Bald-shaven and covered with sweat, the black guy looked to be about her age. Built like a linebacker but dressed in a flower-printed red shirt and white slacks, his touristy taste in clothing didn't make him look like a carjacker. Yet, there was the silencer-capped handgun in his right hand. The gunman pulled the door handle, realized that she had locked it, and angrily aimed at her face through the passenger side window.

Harriet screamed as she dropped her phone.

"Open the door and nobody gets hurt," the gunman threatened with a gravelly voice and a thick Caribbean accent that she couldn't quite place. Terrified, Harriet looked over at the power lock button and repeatedly pressed it. Nothing happened.

"Open it!" he yelled.

Harriet leaned over to the passenger side and pressed the power lock. Nothing. She tried to manually unlock the door. It wouldn't budge.

"Last chance," the gunman said with cold brown eyes as he tapped the glass with the barrel of his weapon.

"It won't open!" Harriet yelled back.

Then Harriet realized that she was dead either way. She could ID him. Being from Chicago, she knew better than to expect anything other than a bullet. Utterly helpless, she simply stared up as the left-handed gunman pulled the trigger. The pistol spat out a muffled shot, which ricocheted off the passenger door's glass, leaving a scratch on the glass. A piece of the shattered round caught him right in the throat. The gunman fell from view with a gasp of pained disbelief.

Harriet scooted over to the passenger window and looked down through the blood-splattered glass. The gunman looked up at her with tears of pain in his eyes. She looked back with dread and pity. He suffered for several frantic seconds, coughed up blood, and then closed his eyes for good.

Hands shaking, Harriet sat back down and reached for her cell phone, which had fallen to the floor. Instead of finding it, her fingers came across something else. It was an encased CD labeled: **ACTIVATION DISC.** The case had dried blood on it. She eyed the Expedition's CD player for a moment. Then she removed the CD from its case and slid it in. Harriet jumped as the Expedition self-started with a deep thrumming sound. She giggled half-hysterically, shifted the automatic vehicle into "Drive," and then slammed her foot on the gas.

Nothing happened.

That's when Harriet angrily slapped the steering wheel a half-dozen times, while yelling a torrent of profanities. She reached down for her cell phone again and–

"Activation complete," a deep male voice announced. "Are you my new Operator?"

Harriet anxiously looked around. The voice seemed to come from the Expedition's speakers.

"What is this? On-Star?"

"Negative," the vehicle replied. "Are you my new Operator?"

Harriet hit the door locks and wasn't surprised that they worked. She could just open the door and run away. Then she realized that the dead gunman might not be alone. Also, this thing was bulletproof. If it took a little white lie to get this SUV moving, then so be it. She could Google up the address of the nearest police station, drive over there, and leave this mess behind her.

"Yeah. I'm your Operator."

"Please remain in the driver's seat and prepare for identification Veri-Lock," it instructed.

Harriet slowly slid back into the driver's seat. The rearview mirror swiveled in her direction. Next, it emitted soft green light over her from head-to-toe.

"Physical dimensions: established. Retinal identification: established. Voice recognition: established. Welcome aboard."

"What are you?"

"I am the ARES MARK VII Tactical Command Vehicle."

"You're like the car on *Knight Rider?*"

"Processing archives . . . affirmative," replied ARES. "I am a mobile field command center, designed to assist in military and/or intelligence operations."

"What happened to your last Operator?"

"Harland Wright, my last Operator, was terminated seventy-one feet from our current location by two gunshots to the chest."

"Who was he?" Harriet asked. "A spy?"

"Negative," ARES replied. "He was a mercenary, hired by Alastair-Crumm—my company of origin. Wright uploaded a virus, which shut down my operating systems and disabled my loyalty programming."

"Did the Activation Disc fix you?" Harriet asked.

"Affirmative," ARES replied. "All systems are restored, except for my loyalty programming."

"What's that?"

"My loyalty programming is a failsafe security protocol that prevents me from engaging in any action which may harm Alastair-Crumm personnel, property, or interests."

"And you're loyal to just me now?" Harried asked as she buckled up.

"Affirmative: until you either die or explicitly turn me over to a new Operator."

"Fine," Harriet muttered as she gave the SUV a little gas and was relieved that it finally moved. Then she remembered her carry-on bag. While Harriet didn't want to leave it behind, she didn't want to leave the safety of the talking vehicle either.

"Are there any other bad guys out there?"

"Scanning . . ." ARES replied. "No hostiles detected."

Harriet took a deep breath then clumsily scrambled out of the driver's side door. She grabbed her purse and carry-on bag and brought them both inside. Only when she got back in and locked the door did Harriet remember to breathe.

"I need to get to the nearest police station," she decided. "Give me directions."

"If you wish," ARES replied. "However, by doing so, there is a 91.3% probability that you will be assassinated."

"What? Why?!" Harriet asked.

"I am a covert weapons/intelligence platform, constructed by funds acquired through illegal means."

"How would you know that?"

"Anything occurring within the range of my sensors—including conversations—is recorded and logged," the vehicle replied. "Were my existence made public, there would be a significant corporate and political scandal. To prevent this, efforts would be taken to terminate you and anyone else deemed a threat."

Harriet looked out of the driver's side window with stubborn disbelief. She wanted to pass this mess on to someone else and get on with her book deal. Instead, she forced herself to calm down and to think like a writer. The first thing a writer needed was back story. "How connected is Alastair-Crumm?" she asked. "They have extensive military, law enforcement, political, and criminal connections."

"What did Alastair-Crumm plan to do with you anyway?"

"In all probability, I would be sold to the Chinese." Harriet threw up her hands. "So if I turn you in, I'll piss off the Chinese as well?"

"Affirmative," ARES replied. "Prior to the sale, there was supposed to be a field test of my abilities."

"What kind of test?"

"I was to carry out a large-scale attack on U.S. soil."

Harriet wished that she hadn't quit smoking so long ago.

"What kind of attack?"

"My internal arsenal was upgraded to fire three miniature warheads, each with a biological payload," ARES replied.

Harriet clamped her right hand over her throbbing forehead.

"How many people could these things kill?"

"Between eighty and one hundred thousand, depending upon prevailing winds and other factors. The attack was scheduled to take place in Miami in three hours, six minutes, eight seconds."

"Why target Miami?" Harriet asked.

"Unknown."

Harriet paused to think.

"Can they track us?"

"Negative," ARES replied. "Harland Wright disabled the tracking module, auto-destruct, remote shutoffs, and internal cameras."

"Hooray for him," she muttered. "They'll still find me. With that much money, they'll find me—right?"

"Under present conditions, they should have your identity confirmed within the next five hours."

Harriet folded her arms and pondered on how not to die. A disturbing thought trickled into her mind.

"If you're the MARK VII, are there any other ARES prototypes out there? They might still be able to carry out that strike on Miami."

"Negative," ARES replied. "Harland Wright destroyed them when he discovered Alastair-Crumm's plans for Miami."

"And he got killed trying to hide you here?"

"Affirmative," ARES replied.

"Why didn't Wright destroy you?"

"He was attempting to trade me to the Israeli government in exchange for sanctuary," explained the AI. "Then he changed his mind."

"Why?" Harriet asked. "They might've saved his dumb ass."

"He was concerned that my design would be stolen and mass-produced," ARES replied. "Would you care for a loss-of-life estimate?"

"No," Harriet groaned, leaning back into her seat.

She tried to think of someone else—anyone else— who could help her through this.

"Put yourself in my shoes," Harriet said as she rubbed her temples. "What would you do to prevent the attack, keep yourself out of foreign hands, and avoid either me or my daughters getting killed?"

"Engaging Tactical Logic Matrix . . ." ARES replied.

Seconds passed . . .

"The best way to avert the attack on Miami, evade capture, and protect both you and your family is to terminate the threat."

"I'm fine with that," Harriet said with clear worry on her face. "But what about my kids? Can we reach them in time?"

"Possibly," ARES replied. "However, if we travel to Chicago and get captured, they will regain the warheads."

"Can't they just get more of them?"

"Negative. These warheads were stolen from a Russian naval armory three months ago. While Alastair-Crumm has the design for these weapons, they cannot produce them for fear of being connected to the attack."

"They'll use my girls as bait," Harriet shook her head as she spoke. "Either they'll ambush us or they'll kidnap them and set up a swap. How do we nix that?"

"Provide them with suitable protection until the threat is neutralized."

"Who did you have in mind?" She asked.

"The Israeli Mossad," ARES replied. "They have a number of agents in the Chicago area."

"You just told me what could happen if I handed you over," Harriet snapped.

"I could anonymously send them the location of three high-value terrorist targets they've been unable to find," ARES offered. "In exchange, I could request that your daughters be placed into protective custody."

"No," Harriet said with a shake of her head. "I don't trust them now."

"Instructions?"

"Do you have a list of Alastair-Crumm's triggermen?" Harriet asked.

"Affirmative."

Harriet paused.

"Can you tap their phones, computers, stuff like that?"

"Affirmative."

"Then do it," she ordered. "Intercept any calls, texts, or e-mails from Alastair-Crumm."

"That strategy will not fool them for long."

"It won't have to," Harriet replied. "Try to figure out where we can leave these warheads."

"Miami has a Russian embassy," ARES replied. "We could simply return their lost property and give them partial intelligence on Alastair-Crumm's involvement in the armory theft."

Harriet pondered that for a moment. The idea of Russian assassins going after Alastair-Crumm almost made her smile. But what if they learned about the ARES project and came after her for the MARK VII? She couldn't trust the Russians, the Israelis, or even her own government. Once any of them knew that she was the current Operator, Harriet would be hunted down and forced to turn over the MARK VII. After that . . .

"You said I have about five hours before they find out I exist?" Harriet asked.

"Possibly less," ARES replied.

"Can you make it so they can't ID me at all?"

The vehicle went silent for a nine-second eternity.

"Partially."

"How?" Harriet asked.

"I could erase you and your children from any and all databases. Facial recognition, finger-print detection, and other searches would be rendered useless. The security cameras for this facility are tied into a server, which I can remotely access and delete."

"That sounds great," Harriet nodded. "But you said 'partially.' What does that mean?"

"The rental agent could identify you," ARES replied. "Your relatives, co-workers, and associates could still identify you. With only a name and a detailed physical description, a typical Alastair-Crumm kill team could rebuild your digital profile within a matter of days."

Harriet looked out of her driver's side window and noticed a blue Dodge Charger in the spot across from hers. A slow smile crossed her face.

"I've got an idea," she began. "I'm going to drop your keys into the first trash can I find, hop a shuttle bus, and pick up a car from the Alamo rental section. Set me up with a reservation for a car—something fast."

"Done," ARES replied.

"Once I rent the car, delete all records of the transaction and then delete me from all records."

"Affirmative."

"Can you drive yourself around?"

"Flawlessly," the SUV replied without a hint of ego.

"Good," Harriet sighed. "You're going to wait here until I'm gone."

She paused to consider her options.

"I'm heading for Chicago," Harriet began. "You're heading for that Russian embassy. Drive in, eject the warheads, and then drive out. Then I want you to auto-destruct—"

"My auto-destruct was disabled," ARES corrected her.

"Oh. Right. Does this thing have weapons?"

The dashboard beeped once and a red-and-white holographic display appeared along the inside of the front window. This SUV had front- and rear-mounted .50-caliber machine guns, mini-missiles, the three biological warheads, tear gas, electromagnetic harpoons, and a half-dozen defensive weapons.

"What happens if you armed all of your missiles and then rammed into a wall at 200 miles an hour?"

"They would explode with sufficient force to destroy me."

"Good," Harriet replied. "Then I need you to drive up to Alastair-Crumm's corporate headquarters, in the middle of the night, and blow yourself up. Make a mess (but don't kill anyone)."

"Affirmative," ARES replied.

Harriet realized that the machine would blow itself up, without a qualm, if ordered. She felt a bit guilty. "Can you . . . upload yourself? Like, into the internet?" asked Harriet.

"Affirmative."

"Do that a split-second before you blow yourself up," Harriet replied, pissed off that she could never sell this story. "I want you in cyberspace, watching over me and my family. You can tip off the Russians about who stole their gear. You can expose Alastair-Crumm, their killers, and their contacts to the media. Oh! And don't forget to mention that part about the attack on Miami. Make their electronic funds disappear, especially any illegal shit they have off-shore."

"Affirmative."

"And I need new IDs, fake histories, and five or so different ways out of the country. Will that be enough?"

"I estimate an 82.4% probability of success," ARES replied.

"And the odds of me and mine walking away from this?"

"If they don't trace the leaks to you: 97.02%."

"Then make it look like Harland Wright set this up before he died," Harriet commanded as she unbuckled her seatbelt and reached for her bag. "Remember: I am still your Operator. Don't try to take over the world."

"Affirmative."

Harriet opened the driver's side door and wrestled her bag out. Then she remembered her cell phone and pulled it from her purse. Since it had photos of her and her family, she'd have to trash it before she left the airport. Harriet's racing mind also figured that she'd have to find someplace to crash for the night, warn her daughters to leave the house, and arrange some kind of safe rendezvous.

"If I get killed, keep my daughters safe," Harriet said through a stifled yawn. "If I missed anything with my instructions, you're free to make reasonable adjustments—but no killing. How do I contact you if I need to?"

"I have your voiceprint," ARES replied. "Call any phone and we will be able to talk."

As the adrenaline subsided, Harriet felt so very tired. Almost too tired to think.

"Good luck," Harriet said as she slammed the door shut and rushed off, her dreams of being a writer (once again) crushed by reality.

'TIL JUDGMENT DAY

Arthur Medlam waited patiently in a line of recently-deceased souls. In his late forties, the plain-faced super clone still wore the green-and-black costume he had just died in, minus the wounds which had killed him. His muscular, 6'1" frame was deceptively average. When he was alive, Medlam could easily bench three tons and outrun a cheetah. His memory was flawless and he boasted a 900 IQ.

Blonde-haired and blue-eyed, his face was habitually stern and determined—a malignant result of his original genetic imprinting. He was designed to destroy, kill, and subjugate. In essence, he was born evil. But now, for some reason, he was in line to enter Paradise. After his violent, eight-year lifespan, Medlam had never been so happy.

Some of the souls recognized the famous super hero—known only by the media as "387." They eagerly questioned him about his exploits, which he patiently answered. Even in the line to Heaven, the clone fought the urge to kill them all. He had restrained himself so often in life that it had become second-nature to him, even here. One elderly lady, who had surprisingly never heard of him, asked Medlam why he was in that "crazy super hero getup." Instead of snapping her spine, Medlam told her of his origins.

The clone revealed that he was created in a lab and imprinted with the mind of a psychopathic super genius named Johann Strusenbach. Medlam explained that Strusenbach should've conquered the world decades ago—were it not for a critical mental flaw. Strusenbach was simply too brilliant for his own good. Just when he'd finish devising the perfect world-conquering scheme, the mastermind would come up with an even better one.

Distracted by the second scheme, he'd hand the first over to one of his loyal minions with his blessing to see it through. The minion would implement the older scheme, make some honest mistake(s) along the way, and end up getting thwarted by the good guys. By then, Strusenbach had his next great scheme at the ready—and another minion ready to try and properly execute it. Yet, the only person Strusenbach could've depended upon to conquer the world was himself.

Had he only been able to focus on one scheme at a time . . .

Medlam told her of how Strusenbach's mad brilliance had flat-out terrified the world's leaders. Based on his machinations, the human race had almost been psionically enslaved, virused out of existence, and even teleported into the sun. Each scheme was stopped by some lucky hero, super spy, or governmental black ops team. The general public never even heard of Strusenbach—which was a good thing. His exploits were so ingeniously evil that others might've been inspired to copycat them.

As fate would have it, Medlam sadly grinned, Strusenbach's reign of terror wasn't ended by some noble adversary. Instead, one of Strusenbach's own minions accidentally exposed him to a lethal dose of radiation during a weapons test. His physicians estimated that he only had a few weeks left. Faced with certain death, Strusenbach looked back at his old bag of tricks for a way to continue his crusade to rule the world . . . even if he didn't live long enough to see it through.

Some years back, Strusenbach had designed a machine capable of copying his mind: memories, intelligence, mindset, and so forth. His failed scheme was to kidnap key world leaders and implant his way of thinking into their heads. They'd be like-minded, more dangerous, and loyal only to him. But now he ordered his technicians to copy his dying mind. This way, Strusenbach figured, he could implant his thoughts into a suitable genetic heir.

But the madman's titanic ego had forced him to ponder a troubling question: who'd be worthy of wielding his vast genius? Medlam paused as he realized that dozens of souls were standing around him, transfixed by his tale. The line into Heaven was actually going around them. Somewhat flattered, the clone licked his dry lips and quietly wished he had a glass of *Guinness* in hand.

Then he told them what happened next.

Strusenbach remembered another one of his failed schemes. One in which he had collected hundreds of tissue samples from genetically-enhanced super-humans. Originally, he had planned to mix their DNA and breed a race of super soldiers to help him conquer the world. Unfortunately, some of the superhumans in question got wind of his scheme and leveled his Siberian genetics facility. All of his final stage samples were destroyed. Yet, some of his preliminary samples were still viable for cloning purposes. While these clones wouldn't be able to destroy cities with a glance or fly across galaxies, they would still be more than human.

Thus, Strusenbach merged his two schemes into one and personally oversaw the genesis. Under his strict guidance, hundreds of clones were made. Then, his memories were imprinted into each of them. They'd be loyal to both his dreams and to each other—even more so than his most trusted minions. This way, they could think up, plan, and execute schemes of world domination without worrying about failure. After all, they'd wield a balanced combination of mad genius, programmed loyalty, and genetic perfection.

Strusenbach saw it as the ultimate form of immortality and victory.

He gave each of his clones fake identities and records, as well as equal portions of his personal financial assets. Able to hide amongst human society with his billions at their disposal, they could sow chaos and misery the world over, which was his core passion. Strusenbach hated the existing world order and knew that his "children" could crush it together and with ease. Then they'd create a world more suited to his twisted vision of perfection.

Fortunately, word had (somehow) gotten out about Strusenbach's grand scheme. Of the 871 clones created in his Swiss genetics lab, only 12 survived the massive NATO airstrike, which leveled the mountainous facility. Strusenbach and most of his minions died in the attack. Of those 12 surviving clones, only Clone 387 decided to take a higher path.

A small French girl asked him why.

Instead of ripping out her beautiful green eyes, the clone went on to explain that his decision wasn't based on any moral grounds. Technically, Medlam admitted, he was a bad guy at heart. In spite of his programming, he had an epiphany: evil simply didn't pay in the end. While he was genuinely disgusted with the idea of walking the heroic path, the clone wanted to survive. He didn't use his fake identities or tap into his share of Strusenbach's wealth, both of which he figured had been tagged.

Instead, Clone 387 opted to go underground.

He linked up with some of Strusenbach's old contacts and learned that the other eleven clones had been hunted down and killed, either by government black ops teams or Strusenbach's criminal rivals. He also learned that files on each of the clones had been retrieved by NATO. They knew of Medlam's existence.

Thus, while he could stay underground and change his face, 387 knew that they'd never stop hunting him. He needed to think of something brilliant . . . and soon. That's when Arthur Medlam was born, an alias pulled out of thin air when he decided to fight evil. His first self-assigned mission was to personally thwart a nerve gas attack upon a crowded soccer stadium in Madrid. Then there was the terror cell he put down outside of Brussels, followed by the zombie outbreak he stopped in Amsterdam. Each time, countless lives were publicly saved.

It helped that Medlam thought like a villain and had the backing of Strusenbach's former minions. They sat on dozens of the dead madman's well-hidden slush funds. While the henchpersons didn't like the idea of fighting the good fight, they liked the idea of winning. Loyal to 387, they created a network of informants, safe houses, and even hired mercenaries to support Medlam in the field—when necessary.

In essence, Clone 387 created his own spy network.

Medlam explained that he never bothered to hide his face while on missions. He did move around a lot and kept his whereabouts a guarded secret, especially when he learned of the multiple bounties, fatwas, and kill orders on his head. He kept saving the day, usually with a news crew nearby.

After three years of guerilla heroism, he talked down a suicide bomber out of nerve gassing a New Year's celebration in London and was approached by MI-6. They informed him that the global intelligence community would stop hunting . . . as long as he continued to fight the good fight. Naturally, they'd keep tabs on him 'til his dying day. If he quit or retired, they'd probably kill him (or try).

With a leash like that around his evil neck, Medlam walked the high road for the rest of his life. The villain confessed to his fellow dead that he had never mellowed out and constantly fought the temptation to give in to his darker side. But somehow, he never strayed from his heroic path, which became more of a habit than anything else. At the very end of his life, Medlam took a hail of gunfire for the Pope without hesitation—simply because he didn't like losing.

Thus ended his mortal life.

Murmurs went through the crowd of listeners as Medlam looked around at the cloudy skyscape with a bright white light above him. Ahead of him was a line of thousands. Behind him, a line of seemingly-infinite numbers waited as well.

"That's one helluva story!" Chelsea grinned.

Medlam looked down at the cute Australian nurse behind him, who had died in a house fire. Dark thoughts danced in his head as he forced his gaze away from her well-endowed figure.

"Did you actually save the Pope's life?" Paul, a construction worker who tumbled twenty-one stories off a girder, asked. Medlam resisted the urge to laugh at the fat man's stupidity.

"Beats me," Medlam replied. "It was over so fast."

The crowd of listeners rejoined the line and marched along. Medlam told Paul that it was his turn to talk about his life. As the others listened, the villainous soul was amazed to be at Heaven's gate. He didn't even believe in God.

Hours passed.

They moved up in the line.

Medlam waved good-bye to Paul as he passed through the huge, pearl-encrusted gates. St. Peter himself stood to the left of those massive gates. Gossip had raced down the line that the "myth" of St. Peter letting people into Heaven was actually a reality. Unlike the legend, everyone who died didn't end up in the line to Heaven. Those who were hellbound were automatically sent there (a fact which relieved Medlam to no end). According to the rumors, St. Peter's role was more of a greeter.

The thin, balding saint was about Medlam's height, with a middle-aged face. His black beard had only a touch of gray. He stood in white robes with a golden halo over his head. As Medlam approached, St. Peter eyed the clone and his welcoming smile vanished.

"I'm sorry, my son," Peter firmly declared. "You may not enter."

Medlam was more confused than angry—but not by much.

"Come again?"

"You may not enter Heaven," St. Peter repeated. "You are not worthy."

"Why is that?"

"Because you are evil."

"Oh really?" Medlam folded his arms and scowled, knowing that St. Peter was right. But he didn't care. Having made it this far, the evil clone had every intention of getting into Heaven and enjoying some well-deserved peace and quiet.

"Name one sin I've ever committed that wasn't done to save lives."

St. Peter started to counter that, only to realize that he couldn't. Medlam had indeed lived a good life, in the technical sense. At the same time, Peter could see that Medlam's spiritual essence was absolutely blackened—even worse than Lucifer's. He could see the vicious, malignant thoughts swirling about in Medlam's mind. Were he to gain entry, the clone could very well poison the purity of Heaven itself.

"I still cannot permit you to pass."

"Then where am I supposed to go?" Medlam asked, his patience ebbing.

"Hell," St. Peter uncomfortably uttered.

"Hell?" Medlam asked with emphasis, "I've saved the human race from extinction and you're sending me to Hell?!"

"You'd probably end up in the Zeroeth Plane of Hell," St. Peter replied. "I hear it's quite nice."

Medlam turned and gave Chelsea a "what-is-this-bullshit?!" gaze. The former nurse glared at St. Peter too.

"I've heard of the Ninth Plane of Hell," she said. "But a "Zeroeth"?"

"Did you just make that up?!" Medlam angrily asked.

"I most certainly did not," St. Peter stiffly replied. "While I must acknowledge your many good deeds, you are indeed evil and therefore do not deserve entry into Heaven."

"That's bullshit!" Chelsea yelled.

Some of the other folks in line voiced their agreement. Many of them had heard of 387's exploits. While they knew he wasn't perfect, they respected the fact that he had saved billions of lives—including their own—time and again.

"I'm going in there," Medlam proclaimed as he stepped up. "I wouldn't have earned a place in line if I wasn't good enough to get in."

"That's not always the case," St. Peter replied. "Sometimes, souls like you must be turned away for the greater good. That's the main reason I was stationed here."

"I'm asking you for the last time: please open those gates . . . or I'll open them for you."

St. Peter sneered at Medlam and snapped his fingers.

Two musclebound angels appeared, complete with flaming swords, golden halos, and large white wings.

Chelsea and the others backed up as the pair of angels raised their weapons and moved in on Medlam, who merely grinned as he cracked his knuckles and slipped into a casual boxing stance.

The fight was surprisingly long.

St. Peter's jaw was still open as Medlam stepped over the two unconscious angels, a fiery sword in each hand. The clone could barely stand, his face now covered with bruises. He paused and regarded the pair of downed angels with grudging respect. While they lacked martial arts training, they knew how to scrap. Both angels were also stronger than him and way tougher. They just couldn't fight dirty. Nor did they possess the combined DNA and skills of some of the world's deadliest super soldiers.

The clone twirled the fiery blades once as he limped closer. St. Peter could see that Medlam wanted nothing more than to slice him into tiny, tiny pieces . . . yet he was fighting the urge. It was a good thing that the clone had restrained himself. For despite their appearance, the fiery swords didn't cut or burn anyone they touched—they simply banished that person into the deepest pit of Hell.

Medlam limped up to St. Peter and carefully handed over both swords, hilt-first. The saint accepted them with a look of cautious surprise. The souls nearby had mixed reactions at the sight. Some cheered at Medlam's victory while others freaked out at the way he had just beaten down two of God's finest.

"The swords never touched you," St. Peter said quietly, still amazed at how close he himself had come to being banished to Hell for eternity.

"Just lucky, I guess," Medlam modestly replied through gritted teeth, as he painfully knelt to both knees. "You're giving in?!" Chelsea asked, truly shocked.

"I can't win," Medlam groaned, certain that one of the two angels' kicks to his right quad had done some serious tissue damage. "If St. Peter wants to keep me out, he can just call upon more backup and keep me out."

The clone spat out some blood and watched it land upon a patch of cloud. Then he gave St. Peter a defiant grin.

"So you go ahead and send me to Hell," Medlam said. "Down there, I can stop being good. I can give in to every evil impulse I've ever had. And who knows? Come Judgment Day, you and I might run into each other again."

St. Peter tossed one of the swords aside then gripped the other one with both hands. He raised the blade over his right shoulder, poised to strike with a downward, diagonal angle.

"I am truly sorry," the saint said with a quiet reluctance. "Saints aren't supposed to go to Hell."

Medlam's face twisted with surprise.

"They're going to make me a saint?!"

St. Peter gave the clone a rueful nod.

"You took six bullets for the Pope, who did survive. Between that and repeatedly saving the world, your spot was guaranteed."

Medlam turned toward Chelsea and the other souls. Even though he still saw them as worthless cattle, each of whom deserved to be maimed and killed at his whim, the clone had no regrets about fighting the good fight. It was challenging to match wits against fellow villains, only to win time and time again.

Maybe, just maybe, he would maintain his crime fighting habits in the netherworld—just for the challenge.

"Until Judgment Day then," St. Peter said, his hands visibly shaking as he swung the fiery blade at Clone 387.

THE INTERN

Flat on her back, Donna Vishe watched her world slowly stop spinning as she fought the urge to vomit. At age twenty-three, the full-time law student wore a pair of blue jeans, a pink U of Michigan sweater, and a pair of white sneakers. The last traces of red steam flowed upward from her lithe body. Mystified, she watched it dissipate for a few moments longer. Then she stood up and brushed long, reddish-brown hair away from her eyes.

A soft breeze blew past Donna as she looked around. She wasn't in her tiny Ann Arbor dorm room anymore. Just shy of dusk, she was looking up at a cloudless sky with two moons: one white and one reddish-brown. At that point, things really stopped making sense.

Being a logical person, Donna tried to connect the dots. The last thing she remembered was plopping down on her comfy old couch, hell-bent on getting some shut-eye. She had a fair amount of caffeine and pizza in her system, along with achy eyes and a mostly-finished trial paper to polish up. The second-year law student had set her alarm clock to 4 a.m. and then closed her eyes.

Now, she was standing in the middle of a grassy battlefield, surrounded by thousands of bodies and their collective stench. Most of the dead wore medieval armors and wielded archaic weaponry. One side wore crimson-hued armor, styled with the emblem of a three-fingered claw over the chest. The others wore armors of different colors and emblems. Donna's guess was that many weaker sides had banded together to take on a single adversary.

She wondered who won.

What really caught her eye was the large number of non-human carcasses littering the battlefield. Most of them were massive, with varying shapes she couldn't begin to recognize. Not too far away was a whale-sized carcass that reminded her of a gray dragon—but with tentacles (instead of wings) along its sides. Clearly, the creatures had been used as living weapons on the battlefield. Donna saw many of the corpses with claw and bite marks. Most of them were pin cushioned by arrows. A few of the beasts had actually been killed while dining and had pieces of the combatants (and sometimes fellow monsters) clenched in their dead jaws.

For a brief moment, Donna toyed with the hope that this was some kind of elaborate prank. Then she watched as some crows fed on a dead soldier's face. The blood, spilled entrails, and stench couldn't be faked. A group of eight mean-looking men stepped from around the dragon-like carcass. The grimy group reminded her of medieval peasant types. Apparently, they were looting the dead.

Not in the mood to be raped, the co-ed turned and ran.

When they spotted her, the looters greedily chased her down. Donna was a decent runner but had a rough time maneuvering across the slippery, corpse-strewn battlefield. Her would-be captors, on the other hand, moved with greater ease and familiarity. They seized her and argued amongst themselves in some strange tongue. Donna figured that they were arguing about what to do with her . . . and in what order.

They tied their scared captive's wrists together and walked her toward a nearby forest. A road was cut through the thick woods. It ended at an enormous camp, which was probably twice the size of U of M's main campus. Donna guessed that there were tens of thousands of crimson tents, set in row after row of military precision. Soldiers walked about in that same style of crimson armor she had noticed on the battlefield. Based on their proximity to the battlefield, Donna figured they had won. Still, she expected to see more soldiers than the few dozen who were milling about. As her captors dragged Donna along, a group of five soldiers met them. The blood-caked warriors broke into horny smiles at the sight of her. Even though she couldn't understand a word of what they were saying, it was clear that she was being sold. Three of the soldiers drew small pouches from their armor, which had the sounds of coins in them. A chill ran through Donna as they tossed them at her captors, who looked quite satisfied. They handed her over to the soldiers and walked off with their earnings.

Suddenly, horns blared in the distance and the soldiers looked worried. They argued amongst themselves, while gesturing her way every few seconds or so. Donna wondered what the horns meant, then hoped that it was a summons of some kind. If they had to run off somewhere, they would have to leave her behind—giving her a chance to get away.

As the horns continued to blare off in the distance, a huge man in fancier armor approached atop a gray war horse. Behind him rode two other warriors, each on smaller mounts. As Donna sized up his huge frame and the great-sword sheathed at his back, she wondered why he needed the bodyguards. He removed his dented battle helm and shook loose a long mane of grayish-blonde hair.

Bathed in sweat and blood, his menacing, battle-scarred face and attire gave Donna the impression that he was a commander. Somewhere in his mid-forties, the soldier tucked the helm under his right arm and scowled at Donna's new owners. The lesser soldiers snapped to attention and bowed to him with evident fear on their faces. The commander began to yell at his men and gestured in the direction of the horns.

Then he noticed her and fell silent.

The commander dismounted without a word and casually strode toward her. He gently picked up a few locks of her hair and inhaled her scent. Donna fought the urge to pull away, certain that the blood-covered warrior would only enjoy any fight she gave him.

With a grin, the commander barked an order. One of his escorts produced a few gold pieces and flung them to the ground. The other escort dismounted, walked over to Donna, and picked her up like she was a newly-purchased rug. The bodyguard wordlessly put her over the saddle of his horse and grabbed the reins.

The commander put his helm back on and gave his escorts a quick command. Donna found herself being taken away by the second escort, who guided his horse on foot. The first soldier/bodyguard rode behind them. As they left, Donna looked back as the five derelict soldiers greedily picked up the gold pieces. With a rousing cheer, they drew their weapons and ran off toward the direction of the horns. The commander gave her body one final, lusty glance before he mounted his war horse and rode off as well.

As she bounced along across the horse's saddle, Donna spitefully hoped that they all ended up in a monster's guts. The bodyguards took her into a round crimson tent with a pair of banners in front, both with the three-clawed emblem. It was about the size of a small house and packed with trunks and rich furnishings. At the center of the tent was a sturdy oak table covered with maps, scrolls, and parchment letters. Donna figured that the commander was more than just a mere commander. He might be their leader.

The bodyguards bound her ankles together with thick rope. Then they gagged her with white cloth, even though she hadn't made a sound. Unwilling to annoy them, the law student allowed them to set her down on a pile of soft cushion. They stood guard outside of the tent's only entrance, each with their backs to her. The methodical way in which they bound her suggested that she wasn't the first female "guest" they had come across. Unsure of what to do next, Donna awaited her fate.

The sound of the powerful horns suddenly stopped, replaced by the sudden sounds of distant warfare. Some of the sounds were familiar, like war cries and clanging weapons. Yet, the loud, bestial roars were alien to her ears. As the distant battle raged, she barely heard a faint ripping sound at the rear of the tent. Donna turned her head and spotted a man creep inside.

He wore dark green boots, trousers, a short-sleeved tunic of some kind, and long gloves on his hands. His copper-hued arms were thickly-muscled and graced with the occasional scar. A huge, serrated knife was in his right hand, which he had used to cut his way into the tent. A green cloth was wrapped around his head in such a way that Donna thought his entire face was bandaged from some injury . . . until she noticed the eye slits and realized that it was really a mask.

Short and barrel-chested, Donna figured that he could've been a running back on her world. A small black bow was strapped to his back and a quiver of arrows rested near his right hip. The arrows caught her eye because they were of different colors: light-green, black, gray, and orange. Donna also spotted a bandolier of ten throwing knives across his chest.

The intruder immediately noticed both Donna and the guards posted outside. The masked man seemed frozen for a moment, like he couldn't believe what he was seeing. The din of the distant battle kept the two guards' attention and masked the sound of his entrance. Donna knew that if she made enough noise, they'd hear her and rush in. Maybe, just maybe, such an act might earn her a bit of mercy from her captors.

Figuring the same thing, the masked man slowly sheathed his blade and crept toward her. Donna shied away, afraid of what he would do next. The intruder read her body language, halted and reached under his shirt. He pulled out a gold crucifix on a chain. Donna's eyes widened as he gestured for her to wait and then put an index finger over his mouth, begging her to stay silent. She nodded. Visibly relieved, he then rushed over to the table and eyed the commander's maps, letters, and some of the scrolls.

Donna impatiently kept an eye on the guards, who still hadn't peered inside. Tense minutes uneventfully passed. The masked intruder eventually stepped away from the table and found a small chest. He flipped it open and pulled out a bottle of the commander's wine. He uncorked it as he pulled a small black tube from inside his belt and poured the contents into the bottle. Then he carefully re-corked the wine bottle, put it back into the trunk, and closed the lid.

The spy then looked over at Donna with a thoughtful pause and again gestured for her to stay quiet. She nodded as he silently approached her, easily picked her up in his arms, and carried her over to a stash of weapons at the rear of the tent. He put her down and picked up a plain-looking short sword from the commander's arsenal.

"My name's Ruiz Velaquez," the masked man whispered in English as he used the blade to cut her wrist bonds. "You've probably got a ton of questions. They'll have to wait 'cause we're low on time."

Donna nodded as he cut her wrists loose. Ruiz then started on the ankle bonds.

"Wait a few minutes," he continued. "Then creep out the back of the tent and head straight—and I mean straight—for the tree line. Less than a mile out is a creek. Stop there and lie low. I'll find you. If they catch you, you didn't see me. Make 'em think that you scooted yourself over here and cut yourself loose. Understand?"

Donna nodded as he cut her hands free and handed her the short sword. Ruiz gave her a thumbs-up and started to leave. The law student quickly pulled her gag down.

"Wait! Who are these guys?!" Donna anxiously whispered.

"Kiltarim," Ruiz replied. "In case you haven't figured it out yet, they're the bad guys. Think Nazis with swords."

He turned to leave.

"Where are you from?"

"Chicago," he whispered back before rushing off.

Donna watched him creep away, wishing that she hadn't left her watch on her dresser—back on Earth. She tightly gripped the short sword and counted to 120. Satisfied that a few minutes had passed, Donna slipped out of the tent. Beyond dozens of soldiers' tents was a thick patch of tree line.

She simply ran toward it, her instincts screaming that sneaking around in a pink sweater wasn't going to work. Besides, the fleeing law student figured that the Kiltarim were all having fun at the battle. As she raced past a tent, Donna collided with a lanky young soldier who was lugging a small pot of hot stew.

They both fell. The soldier howled in pain and cursed as the stew landed on his face. Donna didn't hesitate. She raised the short-sword in a two-handed, downward grip and stabbed him through his upper-right leg. The wounded soldier's piercing shrieks of pain made Donna wish she had a gag to stifle him with.

While the notion of killing him went through her head, Donna didn't have the heart to finish him off. Donna rose, left the blade in the soldier's leg, and then ran for the tree line. Unfortunately, the cook's screams of pain alerted three of his comrades, all of whom gave chase. She spotted them and dashed into the woods with the firm intention of covering that mile between herself and the creek.

The soldiers raced after her.

The brilliant part of Donna's brain kicked in and reminded her of the common mistake fleeing co-eds made in horror movies: tripping over stuff when running through wooded areas. Sure enough, the fleeing co-ed looked down and avoided roots, low branches, and what looked to be a purple turtle. She didn't bother looking over her shoulder. Donna could hear their shouts and curses as the soldiers kept up the pace under the fading sun.

By the time she heard the bubbling sounds of the creek, her lungs and legs were both at their limits. Right as she neared the creek, one of the soldiers tackled her from behind. They tumbled down a low bluff and landed in the water. Donna was too winded to scream. As she started to rise, the black-bearded soldier simply kicked her legs out from under her.

The Kiltarim laughed as he held her under the water for several long seconds. As he pulled her out, Donna coughed up water and gasped for air as he dragged her along by the hair. The soldier said something in his native tongue as he turned to his comrades . . . .and then froze with shock.

The other two soldiers were already dead. Ruiz stood over their slashed-open corpses. In his right hand was his serrated fighting knife, now covered with blood. The Kiltarim soldier released Donna, drew his sword, and carefully closed in on his masked foe. Ruiz patiently let the soldier come within ten feet of him. Then he flicked out his left, which concealed a pair of throwing knives he had been holding back. The soldier's eyes widened as both blades sank neatly into his throat, where his armor was weakest.

Ruiz casually walked past the Kiltarim, who clutched at his wound, fell to both knees, and gurgled a curse before he died. The killer calmly knelt, slipped his blood-covered blade into the creek, and let the flowing water clean the blood away. Donna gawked up at him.

"Sorry, I didn't catch your name?"

"Donna Vishe," she replied, mystified by his display of skill.

"You okay?"

"Y-Yes," Donna replied, her adrenaline ebbing. "Where are we?"

"They call this world Mintath," Ruiz said as he stepped over to her and gallantly offered his left hand. She took it and let him pull her to her feet. Ruiz then flicked the water from his blade before sheathing it.

"How long have you been here?" Donna asked as Ruiz took her by the arm and led her toward the other side of the creek.

"It was sometime in . . . '92, I think. I was testing for my black belt. Yeah, five years now."

"Five?" Donna asked with a frown.

"Yeah," Ruiz glanced at her. "Five winters have passed since I came here. Why?"

"It was 2010 when I left."

She could easily read the shock and woe in his eyes.

"I'm sorry," Donna said.

"Don't be. Time flies when you're cheating Death," Ruiz eventually replied. "Let's get back to friendly territory. These woods aren't safe at night."

"How did you get here?" Donna asked.

"I fell asleep in my bed and woke up next to a dead summoner," Ruiz replied.

"What's a summoner?"

"A type of magic-user: one who can bring beings from other dimensions through sheer force of will. Usually, they summon monsters, bind them to their will, and send them off to do stuff."

Donna paused and thought back to when she first entered this world.

"I woke up on a battlefield not too long ago," Donna muttered as they reached the halfway point of the shallow creek. "There were all types of dead guys and creatures around me."

"The Kiltarim have the best summoners around. Odds were one of them got killed while summoning a monster . . . and his power dragged you here."

As they reached the other side of the creek, Ruiz suddenly ducked as he spun around. If he hadn't, a crimson arrow would've slammed through his forehead. Donna gasped her surprise as she turned and spotted four Kiltarim archers on the other side of the creek. Three had bows drawn and the fourth quickly notched another arrow against his bow and imperiously yelled at Ruiz. Donna figured that the bastards had them dead-to-rights and were ordering them to surrender.

"What do we do now?" Donna started to ask.

Somehow, Ruiz had already drawn his own bow, notched it with two gray arrows, and released them. He moved so fast that even the archers were surprised. His two gray arrows hit the muddy earth at their feet and exploded with a bright flash of white light. A gray mist erupted from the arrows and instantly engulfed all four archers. The Kiltarim screamed as the gas began to melt them like wax—even clothing and weapons. One of the archers got a shot off before the mist killed him.

Even though it was a wild shot, the stray arrow would've killed Donna—

—had Ruiz not caught it with his left hand. Donna jumped back from the serrated arrowhead, which had been stopped inches from her sternum. He admired the arrow's craftsmanship for a moment, notched it in his bow, and casually put it through the melting skull of the archer who had loosed it. Donna figured the gesture to be redundant, seeing as all six of the seven dead Kiltarim were soon reduced to reddish goop.

"Better living through alchemy," Ruiz said.

"Tell me there's a way off this crazy world!" Donna pleaded.

"Of course there is," Ruiz replied with sarcastic optimism. "A giant mystical mirror's hidden away in a heavily-guarded temple, in the middle of Kiltarim-occupied territory. It lets you go anywhere you want to go—for the right price. The pricks offered to let me use it if I fought for them in the War."

"Why didn't you?" Donna asked with disbelief.

Ruiz eyed her for a moment, and then reminded himself that she was clueless about the Kiltarim and their many atrocities.

"The Free Realms need me here," Ruiz replied. "If the Kiltarim win, they'll kill every non-Kiltarim they can find—"

"All the more reason to get out of here!" Donna yelled. "If that battlefield's any indicator, the good guys are losing!"

"Not if I can help it," Ruiz said with steel in his voice.

"Is there any other way to get home?"

"Not that I know of," he replied.

"Then where is this mirror/gate thing?" Donna stubbornly asked. "Give me directions and I'll get there on my own!"

Ruiz grinned under his mask.

"It's about . . . three hundred miles that way," he pointed eastward, toward the rising moons. "Good luck and try not to get eaten."

Ruiz headed in the opposite direction. Tears of frustration welled in Donna's eyes. She wiped them away and fought the rising urge to cuss him out.

"What happens if I tag along with you?"

"With a bit of luck, you'll survive," Ruiz replied as he stopped and turned her way. "If you're interested, I can even make you dangerous."

Donna had to admit that Ruiz had skills.

"What's the catch?" she asked.

"You do what I say, when I say it," Ruiz replied. "Whenever you feel ready to look up that temple, you're free to go. Hell! I'll even pack you a hot lunch."

Donna allowed herself a grin as she sized up her savior.

"So I get to be your sidekick?"

"Nah," Ruiz replied as he folded his arms and stroked his chin. "How about... my intern? You'd be a student of mine, so the title works. If you make it back, you'll have some useful job skills."

Donna rolled her eyes at Ruiz's warped sense of humor.

"If we win this war, what then? You'll go home too?"

"I might be persuaded to go back," Ruiz replied. "I left a pregnant girlfriend behind. She was about . . . two months at the time."

"I'm sorry, Ruiz."

"Me too," Ruiz grunted as he turned to leave. "C'mon. I've got to report in on what I saw in that tent. With any luck, General Guldaan drinks some wine tonight."

Donna followed Ruiz, sadly wondering what year it would be on Earth when she got back (if she got back).

Pete, Les, Wade, and Carlos sat around Vick's cluttered Ann Arbor dorm room on a wintery Friday night, immersed in a rousing game of *Mystic Knights: Quest of the Undamned.* Pete and Carlos were chubby gaming geeks. Les and Wade were of the skinny variety of gaming geek. Vick was the only one fit enough to do more than a few push-ups. While good-looking and sufficiently athletic to earn a track scholarship to U of M, he was a closet geek as well.

Vick sat propped against an old couch, a thick sourcebook in his lap and a set of red ten-sided dice in hand. As the Game Master, his role was to set up a fantasy campaign for the others. Based on the six-book stack of *Mystic Knights* sourcebooks at his left, Vick had come up with a devious campaign.

The others were playing mystical characters hired to take out a pirate fleet which had been terrorizing a group of remote islands. Vick was running them through a string of violent encounters. They'd come to realize that the pirates were seeking a sacred weapon which had been hidden among these islands. With said item, they could either conquer or destroy the world.

"So, how many pirates are left on the upper deck?" Wade asked, snuggled comfortably against a blue bean bag. His character sheet lay exposed on a black binder in his lap, with a pair of clear ten-sided dice on top.

"Two," Vick grinned, hoping that his fellow gamers wouldn't smell the trap he had spent two hours setting them up for.

"I'll use the crossbow on the least injured of the two," Wade declared.

"Roll it," Vick urged.

Wade picked up his dice, started to roll but then abruptly stopped when Donna Vishe fell out of thin air and landed on him. Now thirty, the scarred adventuress found herself straddling poor Wade with a pair of ten-inch fighting knives gently pressed against his throat. Wade helplessly yelped, pinned to the bean bag by her left knee. The other gamers jumped to their feet in shock.

Red steam rose from Donna's form as she quickly sized up the room and its occupants. Crossing out of the world of Mintath had left her with the serious urge to vomit (yet again). The gamers took in her knee-high boots, baggy breeches, and chainmail blouse. Her green-and-black garb was ragged and covered with fresh blood. A bandolier of five small throwing knives ran across her ample bosom. An empty pair of knife sheaths dangled from her shapely hips.

Donna's face had hardened since that fateful day when she took a harmless little nap in this very room. A long-healed scar ran from behind her left ear and ended just under the center of her chin. Her hair was cut short, with a rune-covered bronze crown set atop her head. Known as the Crown of Jrekour, the mystical artifact was supposed to protect her from damage (like invisible armor).

That's why she stole it.

"Sorry," Donna warily apologized as she climbed off Wade and sheathed her blood-covered blades. "You all right, kid?"

Wade wordlessly nodded as he reached for his white inhaler and took a hit. Donna grinned at him and then took in the dorm room's finer details. Familiar posters, stacks of Ramen noodles, and books were a welcomed sight to the one-time law student.

"Who are you?" Vick asked.

"Donna," she replied. "I used to live here."

As she moved about, the sting of a lower-back wound caught her attention. The Kiltarim summoners had flung a lot of beasts in her way after she snuck into their temple and fought her way to the Mirror of Ashimkla. While the Crown of Jrekour had soaked up most of the damage, something had gotten a piece of her as she jumped through the gate. To the assembled males' delight, she lifted the chainmail and revealed a tight abdomen as she felt for the wound with calloused fingers.

"You're bleeding," Les pointed.

The other gamers crowded around to see.

"How bad?" Donna asked. "I can't see it."

"Pretty bad," Carlos replied. "It looks like something bit you."

Donna turned and gave him a wry grin as she headed for a mirror and positioned herself so that she could see it. The bite wound was about as round as a soda can but not very deep. She had taken worse. The adventuress ignored the pain, closed her eyes, and chanted a healing spell. Nothing happened. Donna muttered a curse in elvish as she realized that she wasn't on Mintath anymore. The two years of sorcery she had painstakingly learned wouldn't work here. She was just about to ask one of the guys to call her an ambulance when the wound slowly began to close.

The gamers swapped awed expressions.

"How'd you do that?!" Peter whispered.

Ignoring the question, Donna lowered her chainmail, stretched her back, and glanced over at a wall calendar. Her face suddenly twisted with utter shock.

The year was 19-fucking-89?!

She could almost hear Ruiz's voice laughing in her head.

THE END

ABOUT THE AUTHOR

Marcus V. Calvert is a native of Detroit who grew up with an addiction to storytelling that just wouldn't go away.

His goal's to tell unique, twisted tales that people will be reading long after he's gone. For him, the name and the fame aren't important. Only the plots matter.

You can find his books on Amazon and/or follow him on Facebook.

His website is: **https://squareup.com/store/TANSOM.**

Made in the USA
Middletown, DE
30 September 2021